CW00722999

'Frances Kay's vision of a decimated, dystopian Britain after a modern-day Black Death is both riotously funny and wise to the frailties of humanity. A ruined landscape beset by homicidal tribes, prissy serial killers and priapic Suffolk farmers, seen through the eyes of an itinerant puppeteer, is rendered in roaring, poetic prose. A Swiftian odyssesy that skewers the darkest nightmares of our times.'

- Cathi Unsworth, award-winning author of *The Not Knowing*, *London Noir*, *Bad Penny Blues*, and *Weirdo*.

for May
thank you for
being here!
Love Fan xxx

DOLLYWAGGLERS

Frances Kay

Tenebris Books

Frances Kay 2018.

This book is available in print and e-book from all leading online retailers.

ISBN 978-1-909845-51-0

Cover photograph by Tim Hunkin. Puppets by Meg Amsden
Cover Image Copyright Meg Amsden
Cover design by Ken Dawson
Typesetting and book interior design by Book Polishers

Lyrics from 'Sally Free and Easy' are used by kind permission of the copyright holders of the estate of Cyril & Rosemary Tawney.

Tenebris Books

An Imprint of Grimbold Books

4 Woodhall Drive
Banbury
Oxfordshire
OX16 9TY
United Kingdom

www.tenebrisbooks.com

Affectionately dedicated to
Meg Amsden and Francis Wright
– dollywagglers par excellence

ONE

I AM HAVING A WANK, but my thoughts aren't rhythmic – (strange, the bed hadn't been looted like the others) – up down up down up – remember cooking? Putting dough in pans to rise? Remember bread? – stroking, disconnected; do I feel this? Would I like to? Is it significant?

Under the layers of winter clothes, the old bagman's brown overcoat with holes in the elbows, the agricultural corduroy trousers held up with string, the unspeakable greyish Y-fronts – a grudging warmth is breeding, a feathery flickering of something oily, hopefully sensual . . . If only the nostrils would filter out the stuff that explodes in my brain, as visceral as bowel contents, with the same jocular, offensive intimacy.

Now, there's a word. My hand stops in joyless

mid-gland-stroking. I close my eyes, squinting pig-like along my snout, and turn on my belly.

Outside, it is getting dark. Under a bilious moon, her subjects gibber and puke around the unlit streets, somewhat reduced in number, but for all that, a tribe, a species still.

Face pushed into the mattress, it's easier; I can pretend another hand is fumbling through the layers while I lie, half asleep, half-acknowledging the drowsy spasm that eventually spells release.

Morning has broken and I am woken by impatient, furry dogbreath on my cheek and the feral, faecal warmth of canine canines meeting efficiently around my earlobe. In a masterful (though strangulated) whisper, I establish superiority:

'Hello! Good dog! good fucking boy, down boy.'

Maybe the dog thought I was dead. He raises corrugated eyebrows, then, puppet-like, is jerked backwards, his face comically surprised. I note a glossy studded collar round his tree trunk of a neck. An old – possibly senile – man stands by the bed, his coat the twin of mine, his toothless gob grinning with pleasure; why shouldn't he be happy? The dog has all the teeth this old man needs and, no doubt, some spare brain cells to help out those tricky Alzheimer's moments. At least I know one thing: this ancient gaffer won't be wanting money. (Okay, two things. Or sex.)

'You a Ref?' he quavers. It's a question that requires an answer.

'Fuck, no.'

'Prove it.'

I roll up my sleeves and show my arms. He nods, satisfied. I don't really want to know, but the strange new etiquette of our times demands a response.

'You?' He does the same and I inspect his scrawny inner arms for the tell-tale tattoo, or, more desirably, its absence.

He sits on the bed and the dog begins a soft, low, droning growl, his glittering black eyes fixed on my throat. Oldie, relaxed and powerful, snaps his fingers in my general direction. 'Got any fags?'

I feel in my pockets. Exciting, this lifestyle where one genuinely doesn't know from one day to the next what one will find in them. My fragrant fingers close around a packet. *Fags!* (only slightly damp). Oldie produces matches. We light up, like old front-line comrades.

Dawn has tried to break and we are in the basement of a one-time furniture store. Mine is the only bed left. Oldie, stiff-necked, checks the ceiling approvingly.

'Good kip here.'

'Why didn't they take the bed?'

Patiently, he holds the filthy skirts of my coat to one side, nodding at the mattress. 'Parped on it, didn' 'e?'

Quick as a baby's reflex, I leap up, and the dog, even quicker, has my coat between his teeth. Oldie slaps him playfully over the eyes.

I look down at the mattress by dawn's early light. A faint, viscous outline of a human body merges unspeakably into the ticking. Where last night my comfort-seeking mouth was babyishly pressed, my fingers trace a dried, greenish-khaki-ish stain with crusty edges.

Oldie cackles. 'Had to scrape 'im off in bits. Parped right there, 'e did.'

I take a long drag on my cigarette, feeling the blissful antiseptic smoke freshening my lungs as a young nurse in the dear, dead NHS days used to clean a hospital ward. Breathing out a bedpan of detritus I cough my way, recovered, into the day.

Oldie leads me upstairs to his place, gummily garrulous and far from senile. Somehow, he has the puff simultaneously to monologue and, goatlike, hoof his way upward. I listen to his wheezy resumé, brain in attendance, in case he might give me a memory test later. It's all, of course, about his present situation, and mercifully, it doesn't take long.

We breakfast together on some sultanas, avoiding any references to our pasts; it's the kind of taboo one delicately observes on first meeting, in the new scheme of things. All

I tell him, unprompted, is that I've just arrived in town. Maybe, if the friendship were to ripen, we could exchange names and histories. But I don't intend to hang around that long.

Oldie has taken up residence in a bookshop; after the Eppie, when society as we knew it melted down, only the youngest and strongest holed themselves up in supermarkets and warehouses, wherever the food was. But since he acquired the dogs, he's become upwardly mobile in the sense that people give him whatever he wants. He has a mattress, blankets – even though he doesn't need them, sleeping, as he always does, with a pile of dogs on top of him – matches, attractive rustic-style log baskets of books for fuel, even some wine in the cellar. His other calorific needs are met by a few friendly visits (with dogs) to the new acquaintances he's made who still have access to food shops. He's not as dim as he looks, Oldie. Doesn't take over a food shop himself, because he knows he'd be in a constant state of siege. He'd have to kill a lot of people if he was lucky enough to live in the Sainsbury's collective, for instance. You're only allowed to join that particular élite if you have a gun and a year's supply of bullets.

I could see that if I stuck with Oldie I could learn quite a few life-enhancing skills. He's a little short on contemporaries, most of whom parped immediately, oldies being particularly susceptible to the Eppie, but he's coping admirably.

I halve the packet of fags with him, and in return he arthritically proffers books:

'Whatever you like. Pick of the shop.'

Narrative won't cut it. I crave poetry, the nourishing metaphysical nipple. But he's already burnt the Byrons, Drydens, Tennysons, Wordsworths, and the gorgeously flammable moderns – the paperback Heaneys, Duffys and Hugheses, along with the Shakespeares, the dictionaries and encyclopaedias. Dan Brown, Ian Fleming, John Grisham and other pillars of DickLit, he's touchingly saved till last. They'll go soon, as winter bites down. And thus, all over the world, I imagine.

With absentminded optimism, I select a tiny A-Z of the old, alive London. How Oldie cackles as I tuck that into my rucksack, which holds merely matches, candles, printed emails, a postcard or two, and a packet of dillisk or dulse – dried seaweed from the West of Ireland. Though I'm not Irish, that seems to be where I hail from now.

As I make to leave, I stub my toe on a book, unexpectedly propping up the leg of a moribund fireside chair. It's a hardback, and in the dim light I can't read the title, but who's in no position to be choosy? Into the pack it goes; a tasty surprise for later on, or, more usefully, a firelighter.

Oldie, festooned with disappointed dogs, sees me to

the door. Rottweiler No. 2 gives me a farewell drooling laceration on my calf, easily piercing the dung-stained corduroy, as I wait with old-fashioned courtesy for a parting blessing. The ancient geezer puffs up his skinny chest and clears his throat. It's a nostalgic moment; a throwback to the days of the forties he probably still remembers, when the older generation passed on nuggets of oral wisdom to their respectful young folk.

'If you have to crap, son, dig an 'ole. Don't do it nowhere else. Ain't safe.'

Stupid old fart – he's actually serious. I nod, as one receiving enlightenment, and successfully lift another box of matches from his pocket before leaving.

—

He, the patient, didn't expect it would be very long now. Another cheerful fucking sunrise – why he'd picked this room, where the midwinter sun slanted its long fingers from bullying morning light to sullen, purulent evening shadows, he couldn't remember. Now he was too fucking fucked to move. Maybe he'd strike lucky and go blind soon, as some of them had done before they parped.

A few nights ago he'd had company. They weren't exactly friends, but they knew his name and maybe his face, which was nice for them, because then they knew what to look for.

'Look! It's him!'

'What you got for us, De-esmondo?'

'Look around you, brothers. Nothing.'

'We're not fucking stupid.'

'And we're not your fucking brothers.'

He'd been too tired to bother with fear. 'I don't care who you are. Just do what you came here to do. Kill me, trash the ward, take what you like.'

But that was too much like bloody hard work, wasn't it? People nowadays simply weren't prepared to put in a bit of physical effort to earn their living. What could be easier than shitting on the sheets, setting fire to the lockers and slashing the mattresses in the abandoned hospital?

They grabbed his hands, two of them holding each hand, grinning.

'You tell us, tell us, Des-mond, Desmondo, Dezzy, Dez—'

One of them had looked under the pillow. 'Look who we've got here!'

He practised not breathing. Couldn't they see he was dying?

They began moving his fingers forward and back, gently at first.

'You must be a fucking millionaire. Must have stashed it somewhere. Must have cashed it and stashed it, like it said on the telly.'

'If I had anything, anything at all, you could take it. What can you do with money? No one wants it.'

'You know the *telly*, don't you, Desmond?'

Every time they said the word, they pulled his fingers further. Backwards. Forwards. Apart.

And all the time the little mouth was silent.

I begin to hate the A to Z. It hasn't adapted to the new demands of the situation at all. Of course, I have the benefit of dramatic irony. But somehow, that fails to soothe. As I go south and east, I jaggedly tear out the pages that particularly annoy me. The A to Z is nothing but a self-important museum piece enthusing about dead London as it was, even up to the dying months of last year, bustling with multi-coloured people, traffic, shops and one-way streets. One-way streets! In four days I'd completely forgotten why we once needed them. Only the Underground map with its earnest primary school tidiness still commands my respect, a visual requiem for a city that believed it was immortal.

Some hours later, I found a tube station that was still open. I walked down the steps of Warwick Avenue (I think it was) where the wind always blows and a kindly, hand-scrawled notice still hung there telling you the wind still blew and the steps 'can be dangerous and slippery in wet weather'.

A stiff, black, parped figure in the ticket office showed me hospitable teeth and fingers crooked in a money-taking attitude. I lit a candle and for some crazy reason began to walk clumsily, anticipating movement that didn't happen, tripping, swearing, down the silent escalator, knowing I would have to walk back up again – still can't get into the habit of conserving energy – and stood on the southbound platform. Dead. Nothing. No one. Quiet.

Hands up all you kiddies who were born and raised in London. Remember those recurring nightmares about falling on the tube line? The pulsing rail that hypnotises you to stumble across the steely track, the jolting buzz that shocks you awake? *No risk, no dare*, we used to say, before everything blew apart. It took me all of fifteen bladder-loosening minutes to step down from the platform and put one foot one the rail, even though I knew there was no electricity. Conditioned to a palsy of fear, I could not put my hand on the rail. Not my hand! Not my left hand!

A contemptuous, baby-faced rat watched me quietly as I, farting with terror, stood undecided in the gap which we had always been asked to mind, and then he, or she, skipped along the rail, fixing me with a telepathic eye.

(Black Death, Room l0l, Pied Piper. I had a friend, surely now dead, whose opportunistic burglar father, previous to his life of crime, helpfully had the tips of his baby fingers gnawed off by rats, as a result of which he had no fingerprints.)

I hopped off the rail and scuttled, as much as an overweight person of six foot can scuttle, back up to the platform. Imagining that somehow the rat still played by the old rules, I leaned against the wall, panting. With appalling agility, he followed my route on to the platform, sniffing and frisking towards me. I felt in my pockets for the lovely fags and lit one from my quavering candle flame. At the same time, conscious of a new and nasty rustling behind me, I remembered that I was committed to climbing the escalator at approximately one-third the speed of an averagely fit rodent, keenly motivated by hunger for human flesh. My mouth slacked open and without effort the words of a ghostly song came echoing out. I tried to hypnotise the comedian, the rat:

O the rats have gone and we the crew,
Leave her, Johnny, leave her,
And it's time by Christ that we went too,
And it's time for us to leave her . . .

My words had a richly acoustic, confident resonance which perfectly accompanied my serpentine writhings towards the exit. There seemed to be rats to the front of me, rats to the side of me, rats divinely intelligent, not taken in for one moment by my jaunty sea-faring bombast. Clutching the dead escalator handrail, I dropped the candle. Eerie half-light mocked my wheezy ascent as I topped my performance with a gut-wrenching fart, hoping for a third lung to embody itself within me, to cope with the extra-tarry mucus so often induced by sea-shanties, curse them.

I took my bearings, still in nautical vein, and set sail for what remained of Finsbury Park. Well, assuming the park would still be there even though the concept of Finsbury Parkness, as it had been in the last months of the year, no longer existed. Impartial January sunlight illuminated a London very recently past its undignified death throes. It looked exactly like those images we used to see so often on television representing war. Fires, some still smouldering, replaced houses. Absence of persons – apart from well-behaved, neatly laid out ones decorating the pavements – balanced by the souls of graceful buildings, still impressive, even without roofs or windows. How many centuries of human ingenuity, time, money had been squandered here? What rage had finally taken control, to level and devastate, under whose orders? Can chaos have a leader?

The old grasp of rhetoric was admirably unimpaired by circumstances beyond my control, it would seem.

Without buildings, or even streets in the way, the journey was pleasant and delightful, often accompanied on my part by doggerel folk-type songs to that effect. The odd eccentric humanoid going about their survival business showed a pleasing grasp of today's protocols; mutually, we pretended the other does not exist. If forced to acknowledge another being, such as in this example where I nearly stood on someone's head as he peered down a sewer infelicitously sited on the corner of two still-standing buildings, the following ritual dialogue ensued:

'You a Ref?'

'Fuck off. No way.'

'Fuck off in peace then.'

'Got any fags?'

'Fuck OFF!'

Gangs are a different kettle of fish. They've gone beyond simple theft; the only real shortage is of people. So, some gangs collect bits such as earlobes and testicles, while others try out the waning efficiency of their looted weapons on the skulls of every fifth or sixth random person they meet. The most enjoyable thing about gangs is that collectively, the animal is stupid. It takes them as long to register some novel stimulus as the slowest member needs to engage with it, mentally and physically. Then they argue about what they're going to do next. Usually, they're drunk; having enough alcohol to get langered is one of the ways they demonstrate power and status, so physically they're all a bit blurred, like a huggy old brown bear in a grouchy mood – but it doesn't save me from being lightly done over once or twice, in spite of my size.

What annoys them most is that I won't talk. That's not unusual nowadays, giving nothing away – but I won't make any sound at all, faced with a gang. Because then I would really be in trouble.

If you hear them bullying their way along the road, dive for cover. Gangs don't tend to have dogs – I guess because they can't agree about what name to call them, which is obviously a plus. On the other, or minus, hand, gangs usually have weapons – not guns, which were commandeered early on by the big boys, but knives, axes, ornamental samurai swords, that kind of kiddy stuff. The most volatile and dangerous ones have access to chemists' shops.

Hey, thinking about it, it's not so different from the old times, is it, with gangs? Almost comfortingly familiar. Except for one big difference. You can't dial 999 any more. You can scream, but no one answers.

So picture me here, crouching in an old public lavatory with no doors, listening to another gang roaring past. Am I scared? Beyond fear, my eyes stupidly focus on minutiae unlikely to be of use in a life-threatening situation – graffiti in a foreign language I can't even decipher and a stainless steel dispenser that still has a long and useless umbilical cord of toilet roll protruding from a hole the size of a sixpence – no doubt an award-winning design in the days of cool Britannia.

Then one – probably the leader, the brains, the ex-army cadet, sniffs and I hear the pulpy splat of his gob on the pavement.

'Somefing inn'air. Pisser – you go in.'

'Nah, nah, noh' me.'

'Yer, garn, Pisser. Get in 'air.'

The sound of a boot being applied to Pisser's trousers, and a simultaneous nasal invasion of urine and soiled cat-litter suggests that Pisser is obeying orders. I stand as tall as I can, hunching my shoulders. I am tempted, fleetingly, to squeeze his tiny body, like a guinea pig, snugly against my breast until apple-green snot pours from his nostrils and, with a rattle and a few kicks, he parps. Then we might have the amusing Peter Pan scenario, Captain Hook's dilemma, 'Who will fetch me out that doodle-doo?'

Just in time, reality intervenes. I remember I can't do a cockerel imitation. Or fly.

Pisser eyes me with the circumspect cowardice that's kept him alive so far. He flaps his hand in the direction of his invisible gang, who have strangely fallen silent.

'Fuck me! He's a big fucker!'

My shoulders heave with silent mirth, Edward

Heath-style, and I let rip a macho, sultana-tinted fart. He steps back, possibly impressed.

'E's a fat git an' all! Gotter face like a slug, 'e 'as!'

'Oaright, Pisser, we're comin' in!' With a surge of comradely solidarity, all ten of them press into the narrow entrance of the toilet building. For a moment they are unable to move either back or forward and I bite down an urge to laugh. Then they burst into my field of vision.

I try to look mean. My heart is racing. I need a fag. I need a gun. Leader brings out a meat cleaver, waggling it encouragingly in my face. He has four front teeth missing. This greatly depresses me.

TWO

FOR RODNEY DE LEON BUCKMASTER-TRENETT, there was no other life than his private London. People had always been excrescences, a necessary series of warts to be sloughed off at caustic intervals. But now the thrombosed heart of the City had been excised, allowing Rodney, an amateur micro-surgeon, to perform deft operations, snipping and ligating with twitching lips the tiny arteries of his personal circulation.

He lay in bed, wiping the dreamtime dribble from his rubberduck mouth and surveyed with complacent, tumescent joy the five minions, the chests of drawers grouped about him. Time to get up now and have the first milkless cup of fragrant lapsang souchong, with perhaps half a Bath Oliver biscuit. Fastidiously, he wiped his genitals with a Babyfresh Sofwipe before stepping, dainty as a ballet dancer, into his silk underwear.

Later, after one ritual, another would begin. Each drawer would be opened and the contents gazed on with a connoisseur's or voyeur's lust. Each drawer contained one million pounds in different currencies – sterling, of course, American dollars, Swiss francs, yuan, even euros, (a rapidly diminishing stash of crumpled notes that were, as in every other way, useless – they barely sufficed for starting a fire or wiping the bum) – roubles . . . and other, stranger notes he could not read. But first, for Rodney was a loathsome maggoty pus-bag of habit, it was time for the business that was his pleasure.

He took a few Beanos and a Dandy from the pile on the chaise longue, and slipped into his pocket an anti-mugger spray of the type that ladies used to carry. Then he locked the Georgian door of his exquisite apartment and sauntered into the grey and greasy street.

'Stop laughing,' they had said, but he couldn't. His fingers dangled this way and that, some crooked forwards, some hanging backwards. It was funny. It looked funny. It felt funny. He laughed, and they went away baffled, as people did now, like characters in a play: they exited.

He slept a bit that night, after the pain let him go, and to his surprise he dreamed of Billie. Dreamed of her hair, cut too short as always, sticking up like a boy's, and under it the wrinkled monkey-imp face and the big scornful eyes; so there was something there still, something not ready to die just yet, although most of him was. Overdue, in fact. And when he wasn't asleep, his thoughts wandered – and that was strange, that his mind should be bothered to go on working, fantasising.

If there had been any pills left he would have taken them. He'd have drunk bleach, if there was any, injected himself with air – anything. But there wasn't anything.

Yes – as I predicted earlier, I am in big trouble now.

They haul me out of the jakes and Leader steps back with the cleaver and gestures to a willing little troglodyte with a Stanley knife tucked into his anthropoid palm. Slash. Right through the poor old overcoat. Slash. Through the layers, almost to the skin.

'Wotchoo want?' says Leader to me with schoolmasterly patience. I don't reply, merely spread my hands and shrug; my deprecatory writhings nearly dislocate my neck. Leader takes this badly, almost personally.

'I'll kill you. Oaright?' (I like the way he has a grasp of the rhetorical question.)

'E's a Ref.'

'Garn, cut 'im, Trev.' Sweating, grunting, Trev has a final slash and my right breast flops like a fish through the wound in my shirt.

That surprises them; they fall back.

'It's a slit, a fucking slit!'

There is more to me, obviously, under the surface; but today, a slug-faced slit pretty much sums me up. My androgynous cover's blown now. Think fast, brain. Get me out of this.

I tuck myself back, dignified and still a head taller than any of them. Rolling up my sleeves, I hold my arms above my head like a boxer, inner arms turned out. No mark. I am no Ref. Slowly, amazingly, they do the same. It impresses me hugely. The power of this rite, so new-to-market, so calculated by some civil service mandarin before he parped, is the only rule of law we now know. It's fragile, very new-born. But it's obviously going to be big for a while.

They seem to be intrigued. A slit on her own who isn't a Ref. That's a novelty.

At this point, I would have offered Leader one of my fags, but they've already been tea-leafed and he's puffing contentedly. Now I have time to observe him closely I can see how young he is. Fifteen, at the most. Just a bunch of kids. Friendly and chatty, and incontinent as puppies.

'Wotchoo doin' 'ere, then?'

I find myself saying, 'I'm a storyteller. Want to hear one?'

Of course they do! Slashing people and nicking stuff isn't entertainment like it used to be, it's a career you have to work at, with plenty of ugly competition. And when the business day is over, unwinding can be a big problem. No smartphones, no Facebook, no Twitter, YouTube, telly. No pubs. No DVDs, no Xboxes, arcades, discos. No sex. Just darkness, during which you could be offed at any minute.

Leader smiles, with gap-toothed cuteness.

'Come on. Come wiv us.'

They like me! They take me to their place. I'm touched. It's an old primary school, hardly vandalised at all. Obviously closed down long before the crisis, bolted and barred with maximum security, it's very new to market indeed. (I wonder briefly if there's something mentally missing with this lot. What juvenile gang in their right mind would want to make a school into their headquarters?) I squash myself into a tiny chair and they settle round me, squatting on the brightly painted miniature chairs and tables, as hyperactive and multicultural as a playgroup.

'Do you want stories about gangsters, dealers, rock stars—?'

'—crap, rubbish—'

'—okay, forget those. What about the future—?'

'Fuck the future.'

A pimply boy suggests football, but he's shouted and kicked down with cries of 'wosser point, there's no football any bleedin' more, wosser fuckin point, Stanley?'

Leader comes up with a popular idea – well, that's why he's Leader, isn't it?

'Somefing about "I'm a Celebrity Get Me Out of Here" but on Mars. With air you can breathe – and us there in it.'

Murmurs of approval, and a few friendly rabbit punches all round. I can only nod. If I had feelings, I might pity this little group.

'Celebs. You mean, the dead ones? The real ones?'

'Yer. The ones used to be on Sky News. Miley and the Royals – Wills and Harry and Kate and baby George. Them lot.'

'And you want them not to die? '

There's a slight difference of opinion over this, but Leader wins.

'It's got to 'ave a happy ending.'

'Except the Celebs. They can die. They never cared nuffin' about us,' adds a skinny lad – obviously the weedy intellectual of the group, if such a group allows weeds. 'Not the baby, though. Babies are well sick.' Which I recognise as a compliment, London-style.

I look Leader in the eye. There is a pregnant pause.

'Can I have a fag?'

Ah, the power of the bard, the ancient mariner, that is mine for that brief moment. Five little fists come thrusting towards me, each with its delightful cargo. I accept them all, lighting up the least sucked-on to begin with. And we're off.

Rodney is back in his apartment, frugally sipping tea. He has boiled the water in a small enamel saucepan over an open fire in his Georgian fireplace. He has adapted. However, there will soon be a water problem. Apart from that, his needs are catered for. Oh, yes.

In the dressing room next to Rodney's bedroom, a little boy is reading the Beano. His fair hair flops charmingly over his dirty collar, and every so often, without stopping reading, he wipes his nose with the back of a miniature, pudgy hand. His eyes are wide and blue, and once they were very trusting; now, not so much; occasionally he makes a mistake. After all, he's only eight.

Rodney stands in the doorway, a tired smile on his loose lips.

'Good comic?' The boy nods. 'When you've finished, we can do that little job you promised. Hmm?' The boy nods again. Rodney has a nice voice. Soft, moneyed, slightly lisping.

Rodney returns to his bedroom and gazes over the misty streets of his world. In a minute or two, he will open the suitcase he keeps under the bed. A frown furrows his brow. He goes back to the dressing room.

'What's your name?'

Three

All over what remained of England and Wales, and maybe Scotland too, the New Age bourgeoisie was waking up. Surprisingly large numbers of them had not parped. They themselves put it down to years of rejecting Establishment shit of all kinds (politico-socio-financial, hierarchico-psychologico-educational, familial-economic), eating wholefoods and herbal supplements by the fistful, wearing crystals, meditating, insulating their immune systems thoroughly with herb tea, aromatherapy and marijuana, and basically being in a good connection with Gaia, the Mother, Earth-Goddess, Fertile, All-Knowing, Neutral but Well-Disposed to Alternative Lifestyles.

Others, less charitably sharing their last thoughts before, ironically, parping in the midst of plenty, said it was because them hippies had lived so long in filth they were resistant to any germs, more's the pity.

So, another bright morning dawned for Rose and her tribe at Paradise Farm, and she dressed in her dusky red velvet skirt, put on her jade earrings in the shape of mermaids and some of her favourite crystals and the amber necklace, tied back her long, wavy red-gold hair with a green and turquoise scarf, and went to milk the goats.

In the big playroom a log fire was burning and toys lay scattered on the floor, just like old times.

Jamie stretched and yawned in the big bed, deciding to wait for his elderflower tea before he got up.

Across the yard the chickens scattered, pecking, as Rose let them out. She collected buckets and udder wipes from the dairy.

Afterwards, standing on the hill, she looked across the valley, peaceful in the January sunshine. It was so warm she didn't even need a coat. Then, abruptly, tears rose to her milky-sea-green eyes. Today was Rufus's birthday. Her only son. Born on the nineteenth of January, the year of the big snow. Delivered at home, by a surprised Eithne – her first human birth after fifteen years of delivering goats – who just happened to be passing as Rose went into labour. (But, as they all said afterwards, It Was Meant.)

Rufus had died the day after Christmas, aged seven. And he was mourned and buried, like the others, in the fallow field, with stones carved by hand; loving, pagan-religious inscriptions, fathers' and lovers' hasty farewells.

Rose took a little notebook from her pocket and wrote something briefly. Then she picked up the brimming buckets and went back towards the house.

Clover and Amber were setting the table for breakfast. Only ten places now. Three little ones, seven big ones. They were giggling in the way that fifteen-year-olds do, but they stopped when they saw Rose's face.

'What is it, what's happened?'

She sat down at the kitchen table, glad to have the feel of the warm elm wood under her hands. Clover brought her some fennel tea. They were making toast and porridge. Familiar, comforting routine. Rose put her head on the table and cried.

~

Now the little boy, whose name is Ben, is lying strapped on a table. He began not liking this very much after he'd finished reading the comic, when Rodney told him to take all his clothes off and fold them neatly. Now, he can't move his arms or legs. Rodney is very gentle and precise in his movements, and his face sags with a soft, creamy quiver that Ben hopes is kindliness. In the old days, of course, he learnt at school about going with strangers. But these days, everybody is a stranger, and those rules don't work any more. You have to go along with strangers now, if you want to eat and somewhere to sleep, and the price is usually a kick or an errand or you have to do something humiliating, and sometimes it hurts. But this, now, this is different. The leather straps are tight enough to make him understand that he is a prisoner.

Rodney is busy at a table, clinking metal things. When he turns around, his hands are empty. He is smiling. The mother-of-pearl buttons of his trouser fly have come undone.

'Ben,' he coos, and licks his lips, and Ben can see the wet stuff glistening on them, 'have you ever wanted to be a little girl?'

The fair fringe flops to one side, then another as Ben vehemently shakes his head.

'Oh dear, what a pity. You see, Ben, I like making boys into little girls. I can do magic. I can turn you into a little girl. Wouldn't that be fun?'

'I don't want to be a girl. Let me go. Please, mister . . .'

'I don't think you understand yet, do you, Ben?' Rodney turns back to the table, and this time his hand is not empty, but curved around a long, pure blade that makes Ben's heart dance with fear.

'Just ask me nicely. Please, I want to become a girl.'

'But I don't—'

'Think of it as a game. Oh, Ben, what have you done!' The blade points a reproachful finger towards his belly. Ben looks down, horrified, and blushes. He has wet himself. Warm and ashamed, he waits for his punishment.

My story goes down like a bulimic's dinner: they gobble it in chunks, can't gulp it down fast enough. They cheer at the happy ending, where their gang rescues the baby prince and finds a palace to live in on Mars. Ah, let's hear it for happy endings! They sit gazing at me, limp, post-coital, dreamy. But as the last words fall into their gape-mouthed silence, I see danger. The old Scheherazade syndrome. It's my cue to take some unpredictable initiative, keep'em guessing.

I stand up, and point at Weedy, the Intellectual.

'Give me your coat.' He's about my height, (thinner, of course, isn't everyone?). Reluctantly Weedy eyes Leader.

'Come on, I haven't got all day—' (though actually I have; we all have now, but I do have appointments, curious as it may seem) '—give us the coat. You can score another one easy enough, can't you?'

Weedy hesitates, and then demonstrates the intellect I've already intuited.

'I never cut yer. Was Trev, wannit?'

'Look, you lot. Do you want another story or not?' Appreciative, gobbling cries indicate an affirmative here. 'Then make him give me the coat.'

With a little force the swap is done, and I'm now the owner of a rather too tight mid-calf length Swiss ex-army coat, tasteful grey-blue with poncy wide lapels.

'Same time tomorrow, then.' I begin sidling towards the door, but Leader has copped on, he's mentally agile, and he's in front of me with that assertive little tool, the cleaver, waggling away like there's no tomorrow. Which, of course, for people in our current mode of life, there can't be really, can there?

''Ow do we know you'll come back?'

'You don't, do you?'

He gives me a hesitant nudge with the cleaver, blunt-end on.

'But if you don't let me go, if you use that thing on me, then what do you get?' I tap my head impressively. 'There's plenty more stuff in here. But you won't see the stories, the words, if you split my brains with that thing. You know yourself. You've seen the insides of a few heads by now – you must have.'

Leader lowers the cleaver, diplomatically checking my pockets so as not to seem weak.

'Come back, eh?' He trusts me . . . I wink, I roll my eyes. The marvellous ambivalence of my body language lulls his pre-teen suspicions.

'Oaright. Laters, Sluggso.' Extraordinarily, he extends his hand towards me. We shake, foreign and wary as the extra-terrestrials my story briefly transformed us into. Then Sluggso takes her leave. They even let me keep my rucksack.

My self-inflicted appointment is at 39 Chestnut Ave., Finsbury Park. I don't know the house, I've never been there, but just before the present unpleasantness breezed in, I received a postcard bearing that address. Chestnut Avenue used to be near Tollington Park, according to my A-Z; a wide street now barely distinguishable, like the stain on the mattress, a tired overlay of rubble in order of meltdown with the ruin of the old railway bridge slashing blackly across it. Beyond, a pale sun-flecked landscape where a few middle-aged figures are moving to and fro with wheelbarrows, purposeful as dungbeetles, but not as lovable.

Number thirty-nine no longer exists, as such; just a plot and a mixed mound of interesting, though slimy, remnants. A random thought occurs that it was a last-ditch attempt of the old government to try and blow the virus to smithereens that has resulted in so many flattened streets. Didn't do any good, though.

It's been raining recently. Patiently I begin sifting, trawling through these dead strangers' effects. Wheelbarrowing figures occasionally eye me from a distance. I try not to look successful.

So what was it about 39 Chestnut Avenue? Why did he, my one time friend, the correspondent (and I choose this double entendre with ironic exactitude), leave his pied-a-terre at Shepherd's Bush – so handy for the Central Line, White City, North Acton, the entire BBC in fact – and retire to this downmarket Vic. terr. 2 bds., g.f.c.h., smll bk gdn, pkng on quiet residential road . . . very, very quiet now, but not so residential . . . ?

Sitting on an upturned armchair, possibly Habitat circa 2002, rucksack comfortably tucked on my ample knees, I scrabble with muddy fingers through my collection of printed communications.

Of course, Reader, you would know about emotional baggage; the type of person who'd be interested in my tale might have been in happier days, if not a practising therapist, at the least 'doing some serious work on themselves with this brilliant past-lives woman in Crouch End'. Well, this is the sum total of my emotional baggage (and it fits comfortably into one small rucksack! I'm either lucky or very dishonest, eh?): here's a postcard from . . . let's call him a guy I used to know. We worked together. Worked and played, you could say.

He writes a beautiful italic hand, so flawless it looks as if it's been done by computer – but it's his own, as always, no doubt using his favourite old-fashioned ink pen.

'Looks like little Desmond is for the chop – I can hear you laughing. Okay, maybe Plan B would have been a good idea. Too late now. I've moved to the address other side. Hope Ireland works for you . . .'

I thought this address had to be another new 'relationship'. But, pursuing subtext, there's a small admission, a minute apology tucked in there. Plan B was mine; Plan B was what I used when words failed us and everything was solved by travelling fast and thinking not at all. Plan B got me free, away to Galway.

'Too late now'; that has a kind of doomy, ungrateful ring about it, doesn't it? Not what you'd say if you'd shacked up with the new love of your life, surely?

Bad news about Desmond – but I never liked that kid, anyway. And there were threats to Desmond's life before, plenty of threats; and once upon a time we might have sat up all night with a bottle of whisky, nearly crying as we worked out how much money we stood to lose if Desmond parped. Notice I say nearly crying, but not quite, because Guy and me, we were unusual in that way. We didn't have feelings, as such.

He signs off tersely with 'Luv, G.' Not even a few XXs to back it up. I light my final fag and cough, or laugh, or something, over this valediction.

It's disappointing, but there really isn't anything to find here at number thirty-nine – no clues, mementoes, knick-knacks. Nothing I recognise as belonging to Guy. No parped and blackened bodies – if there were, they've probably been eaten by man's best friend. Or rats. Or other people. Chaos does strange things to one's dietary habits.

Looking up, I see three beings wheelbarrowing grimly towards me. They've probably got rights of piccage and pokage and rummage. One of them speaks:

'Looking for something?' His voice is civilised; not friendly, but civilised. Christ! He's wearing a dog collar!

I adopt a harmless, sad, religious expression.

'No. I'm only saying goodbye to a friend.' My gaze travels over the three wheelbarrows with a nauseous suspicion that they are gathering bodies for Christian burial, but not so. They seem to be going big on blue. All kinds of blue objects are tumbled indiscriminately on the three wheelbarrows. The vicar's wheelbarrow is the emptiest – maybe he's got a bad back.

'You're not from round here, are you?' says a beak-faced woman in a black hat who could have stepped from the vestry of a church – except that she's wearing rigger boots, and they're spattered with blood. Not from round here! Words fail me. Rapidly, I shred the postcard and scatter the bits over the rubble pile. The vicar has a strange expression on his face . . . maybe the words of a funeral benediction are whirling inside his hairless pate.

'So – how's the Jesus business?' As soon as the question was out of my mouth I could have bitten my tongue off, but he doesn't take umbrage. He gives me a twisted, intelligent smile. I notice how thin his lips are, and how his hooded eyes take on a fleeting resemblance to a species of small raptor. Before he has time to answer, the third wheelbarrow, her generous jowls trembling with loyalty, cuts in.

'Don't waste your time talking to him, Vicar dear. He's just a filthy ref. Needs a jolly good bath, if you ask me, his face is positively grey . . .'

I ignore her, and address the vicar again – I know it's sexist, but it serves her right for assuming I'm a man.

'Can't you keep your flock under control? Can't you all mind your own fucking business? Did you live in this house? Do you know who lived here?'

Jowls responds immediately, 'I used to live in this house.'

'You are a lying, nosy, toad-featured wanker.' I say without premeditation.

'How dare you, you nasty criminal – addressing me in that . . . insulting—'

I kick some clotted rubble in the direction of her stumpy calves.

'And your crony is a shitbrained, necrophiliac vacuum-cleaner—' I observe, then stop. The vicar is enjoying this a bit too much. He's back in familiar territory. Give or take a little robustness in our style of dialogue, we could be arguing about the church flower rota. I address him again.

'So, okay. You're a vicar. You've got the hot line to God. Explain this to me.' I gesture at the general devastation. 'Why? What did we do to get Him so upset? And who's going to triumph in the end, good or evil?'

Jowls and Black Hat, alert for his response, stand respectfully silent by their wheelbarrows, twin pallbearers at the funeral of civilisation as we know it.

'How the fuck should I know?' says Vicar with simple dignity. 'And if I knew, why the fuck should I tell you?'

He reaches into his pocket and stuffs a flyer into my hand.

'TUESDAY JANUARY 28th. RAINBOW JUMBLE SALE,' it reads. 'IN AID OF CHURCH FUNDS.' It is printed by hand in marker-pen rainbow colours; the spelling is faultless. Incredulously, I let it drop, and the Vicar suddenly whispers, urgent and serious and almost certainly insane:

'Life goes on. You see?'

'Funds, what funds? Money's useless now.'

Jowls has had enough of this disrespect. Heftily engaging with her wheelbarrow, she gives a Valkyrie-type cry and directly targets my solar plexus. I hop comparatively nimbly behind the pile of rubble as she veers off to the left, steering hopelessly out of control, squawking like an enraged chicken, fetching up entangled with the old Habitat armchair. As she lies sprawled in the mud, I see with immense delight she is sporting old-fashioned pink interlock knickers.

Vicar, like many mad people, is right. Life goes on. I offer to help her up and she shakes me off, giving me the born-again evil eye. Black Hat dusts her down, uttering wren-like chirrups of consternation.

Ah, the bird life of London!

~

Ben doesn't feel warm any more, but chill. It seemed to start in his insides, this chill, and it gradually worked its way out, until his skin began to tighten and crawl with goose-pimples and finally to go quite cold, as cold as his bunny had been after the cat got it. And he thought screaming might help – but Rodney didn't like that at all, so now he has a pink chiffon scarf stuffed into his mouth and he's scared he's going to be sick.

'This won't hurt very much,' Rodney says, and he looks and sounds just like a doctor, except for the little dribble of wet stuff that runs over his thick bottom lip; he doesn't bother to wipe it away and it drops in a long drooling scribble onto Ben's chest. Rodney has some cotton wool in his hand and he brings this hand gently up between Ben's spread legs and wipes him as tenderly as a mother, and a painless sensation of coldness and blurry, cotton-wool numbness begins to spread down there. Ben wishes Rodney could wipe his mind to numbness like that, and his memory; then perhaps he could go to sleep until it was all over.

'Ben,' says Rodney, 'remember, you asked me to make you a girl. This is what you wanted.'

Which is true. It seems like a long time ago now that Rodney had made those soft, insistent demands, that became more and more intense, more weird and therefore more scary. The voice kept saying it was a game. Ben doesn't know what kind of game this will turn out to be; all he knows is that when he gets out of this he will never go home with a stranger again, even if it means he starves to death.

Rodney puts down the cotton wool and fumbles with his flies, and only then does Ben see the triangle mark on his arm and he knows. Rodney is a ref. He tries to close his eyes but they open all by themselves, wider than ever.

Now Rodney has the scalpel and he draws it up, in one skilful movement, up and in.

Ben wishes he was dead.

⸻

It is later now, and Rodney is kissing him, pulling the pink gag from his mouth and kissing the dryness away with his soapy tongue . . .

'Quite beautiful . . .' he whispers. 'Can you hear me, Ben? You were the best girl of all.'

Strapped down, Ben does not wipe himself, as Rodney does now, delicately, lips pursed, dropping the sopping crimson wad of paper into a box on the floor and doing up his trousers. Ben does not move, even after Rodney undoes the straps and tenderly strokes his arms, patting his face with lilac-scented fingers to wake him.

'Oh, Ben, you seemed to have left me already,' he says regretfully, 'and we had such a lovely time, didn't we? I wish you'd stayed with me longer.'

⸻

Gwyn was scowling into his porridge. He had the bit between his teeth again. No one could be bothered to argue with him – but that had never stopped him before.

'All I'm saying is,'—he eyed Jamie with his traditional, humourless, Celtic intensity—'how do we know our animals won't get it? They told us humans would be immune, didn't they? After it jumped species and everyone queued up for their shots, what the fuck good did it do them? So, all I'm saying is, how can we be sure our goats won't start manifesting signs of disease at any minute?'

Lally poured another cup of peppermint tea and sighed. Gwyn was just so exhausting in the mornings, but as the day wore on his usefulness quotient increased. This energy born of anger, so superfluous at breakfast time, applied to the generator and the well-digging and the chainsawing and the cannibalising of bits of old machinery to make new and useful gadgets, was as vital to their community as her own meditational massages, Jerry's intermittent clairvoyance, Rose's cordon bleu cooking or Jamie's tunes. Besides, Gwyn could dowse water. In present day society, Gwyn should be king.

'If our animals were going to get the Eppie, they'd have got it first,' said Clover, who had been studying GCSE biology before the collapse of society into its component fragments, 'because they're smaller and their cycles go round quicker.'

'No, they wouldn't,' weighed in Amber, who always disagreed with Clover on principle, 'because they wouldn't catch it in the same way humans did. Animals would have to wait until it worked its way down the food chain, like pigs eating dead bodies or something—'

'Shut up,' Rose said, staring at no one, and her mouth was a tight grey line. Everyone was surprised into silence.

'It's someone's birthday today. Would have been.'

'What day is it, then?' asked Lally. Without her mobile or *The Guardian*, she was lost, absolutely lost.

Clover chirped, 'I know, it's January the nineteenth, Amber's made a calendar for our bedroom wall—'

'Oh yeah, you're right. It would have been Rufus's birthday . . .' A shadow flitted briefly across Jamie's eyes, and he took a reverent drag on his spliff. 'Sorry, Rose. We haven't forgotten.'

'I want to do a sweat lodge tonight. For Rufus. For all the dead babies.' Rose felt herself beginning to shake. She looked for help to Gwyn. For strength. For kindness.

'Good idea,' said Gwyn, and reached across the table. He took Rose's hand in his chunky, hairy fists, and squeezed. Looking at him, she was glad to see tears in his dark eyes.

'I'll split some logs.'

'Yeah, cool. The lodge needs a few poles, I'll see to it.' Jamie stubbed out his spliff, ready for business.

'We'll do some smudging, too,' said Jerry, who was lying on the old sofa reading *Country Living* dated November – one of the last to be printed. 'I'll pick some herbs at midday. Has anyone got the right time?'

'God,' said Lally, 'I so miss Radio 4.'

Sally is an unusual nurse, a frowsy, witchy, explosive soprano one; she lives a lurking existence in Clapham. She was my next port of call; she was the printed email in my rucksack:

'Subject: re parps.

'Good question. It was a gutless junior Minister suddenly promoted to take charge of the crisis ('There is, of course, no crisis as such; no need to be alarmed.') who, in the middle of a TV interview, got his tongue in knots and offered 'parped on' in place of 'passed on', following it up by actually parping on the studio floor a few minutes later. The interviewer couldn't help commenting: 'It looks as if Reggie Dukes himself has – er – parped.' A day later, everyone was parping . . .'

Yes, it would be a tonic to see Sally again. She was never the despairing, introspective type. She would make me laugh if anyone could; she could show me how to survive wittily, and even though this time she wouldn't be able to offer me the elegantly slender spliffs or the disgraceful Lambrusco that were her usual poisons, we could party, in spite of everything, because I couldn't believe the Eppie would have changed her the way it seemed to have changed me. I found myself hoping, even offering up a pagan prayer that Sally was still alive.

Leaving God's army ferreting in Finsbury Park, I headed south, thinking it might be fun, in a twisted sort of a way, to pass the majestic old arsehole of the former government. Cowardly misgivings tugged my sleeve as I got nearer Westminster; any real hards, loopers, power-trippers, or axe-grinders who survived would of course be competing to exercise their new democratic muscles in the mother of parliaments . . .

But my fears were groundless. Westminster was as silent as the tomb. Outside the gates, where tourists were alternately fleeced and photographed in the old days, was a tramp-type bloke of indeterminate age I recognised from Channel 4 documentaries, articles in Sunday papers (didn't he used to write the 'onlymanisvile' blog?) and now, real life. His pitch used to be at Oxford Circus station where he paraded with a placard saying MEAT IS MURDER.

'Anything happening in there?' I queried. His wandering gaze came to rest on my earring, a discreet gold sleeper.

'You're all murderers,' he replied softly.

'Okay. Well, not totally okay. But hey – great to hear your opinion. And how about them?' I gestured at the dear old House of Commons.

He raised his voice a fraction. 'In there. All the murderers. You too. I can smell it. The taint of meat is on you.' Which was unfair, considering that my last sausage had been consumed weeks ago, thoughtlessly, in a pub in Galway.

I moved as though to pass him, and he made a balletic little skip to re-establish our original relative positions. I hopped sideways; he did the same. I jigged to the right; he mirrored me. His agility, hampered by the weighty and unbalanced wooden sign around his neck, was a sincere tribute to a life of vegetarian abstinence. However, I was out of puff, so I backed off and looked for another way in.

I had a fancy to see the leather benches, green as pond algae, cleansed of their usual denizens – primitive, mud-burrowing, cannibalistic organisms – and the thumpable, stately dispatch boxes behind which so many plump bottoms have doughnutted for the camera.

The doors were wide open, and in the stone corridors the winds of January blew infinitely colder than outside. Global warming, no matter how extensive, cannot reach the frozen body, or botty, politic.

At last I reached the lobby, where two or three ten-year-olds were rapturously skateboarding on the marble mosaic, and headed into the chamber. An unexpected scene met my eyes: three or four dishevelled politicians, handcuffed together, blindfolded, were, it seemed, just about to be shot by an impromptu firing squad. They were lined up in front of the Front Bench, regardless of party persuasion, and maintained a dignified silence, except for one who was sneezing a lot.

Leading the firing squad was a suavely rotund man dressed in Army uniform, but the seven rifle-people had no designation, no identification. One wore classic, shiny black dominatrix gear; one was dressed as a rabbit; one seemed to be Count Dracula, another wore a mortar-board and gown; two women were dressed like Marie Antoinette. All their faces were concealed beneath grinning carnival masks.

At the order to fire, they fired. Real bullets, it would seem. The politicians crumpled, twitched, and sagged to the ground, in a manner familiar to devotees of leftwing arthouse movies. Then the eyes of the squad turned towards me.

'Like to join us? Always happy to accept new volunteers. You provide your own costume, of course.'

I sought out the lowest vocal register at my disposal. 'Sorry, don't have a gun.'

The leader shook his head, managing to smile without conveying a vestige of humour.

'Weapons will be provided. And you don't need training to hit a sitting target.'

'No, absolutely. Er – well done. Do you mind if I ask a

question? Why the fancy dress outfits?'

'Dying without dignity. The power élite made a laughing stock of us; now their executions have become simply a circus act.'

'Jolly good idea,' was all I could think of.

'But you don't want to actively participate. Sure? There are fringe benefits?'

'Definitely not. But thanks.'

'Then bear witness to the world, brother, that our service to the community continues,' suggested the rabbit. I nodded as agreeably as I could, my eyes drawn to the oozy, twitching, blindfolded figures. A skateboarding kid whizzed in, applauded briefly, and whizzed out again.

'That will do for today,' said the officer, who had a most unmilitary posture: he looked as if he should have been stretched out in a tubby armchair in front of a blazing log fire at his Club. 'See you all same time tomorrow.'

The squad lifted off their masks and filed out loosely, chatting. The officer type went out by a different exit. I drifted out with the firing squad.

'Shot many, have you?' I asked. They thought they had, quite a few.

'All politicians?' They thought so – well, mostly. Troublemakers, anyway.

'Got many more to shoot?'

One of the Marie-Antoinettes took umbrage. 'Are you a journalist? Because we've shot a few of your lot, you know—'

The rabbit soothed her, patting the stock of her rifle with his fluffy paw.

'There's no tabloids any more, my love!'

'We shot them first,' offered the dominatrix, 'and they made a frightful fuss.'

'And we've another long day tomorrow – we're clearing the House of Lords, I think?'

'No, the Bank of England, isn't it?'

'I'm terribly sorry,' I said. 'I didn't realise how hard you're all working.'

The rabbit patted my shoulder. 'The fact is, we simply carry out whatever Brigadier Jeffryes suggests. He seems to know where to find these undesirables.'

'I get it, blooming marvellous – but what's in it for you?'

The rabbit smiled. He had the teeth of a rabbit too, and they weren't part of the costume. 'The satisfaction of knowing that we're doing a public service.'

'And we get to sleep in the bunker . . .' muttered the school master.

'The what?'

Rabbit did something intensely painful, which I didn't see the details of, possibly involving testicles.

'Nice talking to you,' he terminated, pulling the others

along behind him like a row of ducklings, 'mind how you go, eh?'

~

South of the river. On Sally's street, Raglan Street, a few pecked-out windows stared eyelessly into the gathering dusk. Doors swung open and clapped out a listless, off-beat rhythm as I stood uncertainly on the doorstep. A few relaxed rats waddled homeward, the businessmen de nos jours.

I tapped timidly, then knocked peremptorily, then kicked incompetently, then found a doorbell and leaned long and hard on it, to be rewarded by the synthesised chimes of *Ave Maria* (her landlord's choice, presumably).

Assuming that she was still alive, and only temporarily absent, burgling my way in would not be the action of a considerate friend. However. Could we assume anything in these protean times? It seemed regrettable, but serious breaking and entering was my only option.

As night fell like a budgie's blanket, I groped around unenthusiastically for a brick, or similar missile, but happily chanced instead on an upturned flowerpot. Underneath – I've shared a flat with Sally before, I know her little ways – her front door key is buried, invisible.

Inside, I sniffed signs of recent occupation. No whiffs of any parps, either, which was a relief to the olfactory senses. I sank into an armchair, but soon sank out again, realising that I was terminally cold. I pulled a leg or two off one of Sally's ugly and badly-made kitchen chairs and created a fabulous botty-warming blaze which also illuminated the kitchen in a cosy way. No sooner had I positioned the relevant anatomy closer to the fire than I heard footsteps coming up the path. I got behind the door with a raised leg in my hand (chair leg, naturally).

It was Sally, struggling with two bulging Asda carrier bags, and she gave me the sort of guarded welcome you might expect if you had interrupted a hamster before it had had time to stuff its cheek pouches full of nuts. I was hungry. I could scarcely disguise a reflex interest in her 'shopping'; nor could she. We chopped up some more furniture and got the fire warm enough to do a spot of rude cookery.

As she rolled up her sleeves to wash her hands in some greyish recycled water, my eyes were drawn to her inner arms. Silly, I know, but I might have expected Sally to have refused the jab, to be a Ref. She intercepted my look and spoke briskly.

'I had it done. It was either have the shot or collect your cards – at the time you still needed old-fashioned money to buy things and a pay packet was, you know, the best way to get hold of it.'

She plied a tin opener, gritting her teeth.

'What about you?' I showed her my tattoo-free arms. 'So, you had the shot too?'

'Ireland wasn't quite so organised. We died. Or we were immune. No triage.'

'You know how it turned out here? Those shots were useless – worse than that. Made us all quiescent eunuchs.' She sounded as brisk if she was reading from an official news bulletin.

'Yes, I know it made fucking into a mere metaphor, but what about Refs? How did they get chosen?'

'It's unlikely you'll meet any.'

'But if I do – what are they? Goodies? Baddies? Maddies?'

'The government said everyone had a free choice. You could have the jab or you could be a Refusal (and probably die).'

She faltered for the first time. I saw her looking hard at a closed cupboard. Then she snapped herself upright and stuck her chin out, as her voice took on the sardonic edge of the old Sally, a robot replica of the old Sally.

'The first two weeks the hospital did fantastic business. The only way we could move along the corridors was by treading on people's faces. And they loved us! It took their minds off the panic, the plague hysteria. (Of course we weren't allowed to call it plague. First it was 'rodent-borne flu', then 'the epidemic', Eppie, for short . . .) Then the . . . the demand died down. We got sent the straight weirdoes, the politicals, the New Agers, and some genuine refugees. We had to separate them and put them in a side room 'to fill in a form'. They got the tattoo. No one told them anything.'

'*You* had to tattoo them? I thought the police—'

'We did everything. Went on obeying orders until there wasn't anyone left to give us orders. Before the triage started it seemed like there was some kind of repulsive system to the thing. Then, suddenly, chaos. Dying doctors, surgeons, put out in the hospital garden without a blanket over them. Dustbins full of dead babies, not even time to bag them up. And I realised I was one of the lucky ones; naturally immune, I mean, because other nurses and doctors were dropping like flies. I hadn't needed the shot. And it didn't do them any good at all.'

Sally offered me some tinned pineapple. It may sound callous, but I ate heartily.

'Some soldiers appeared and all the tattooed ones were rounded up and taken away to holding camps. Oh yes, from the very beginning we had lists of people who were considered undesirable. They weren't to be given the shot, even if they wanted it. They got sterile water and a tattoo. What an ideal opportunity for skimming off society's scum.'

She finished the pineapple.

'Want to hear more? There's plenty.'

'I'd rather eat more.'

After we had gorged on a packet of ham and pea soup, reconstituted with pineapple juice, cream crackers, and tinned chicken chunks, followed by drinking chocolate stirred into some Ideal milk, we drank metallic-tasting jasmine tea. In order to prepare this simple yet nourishing meal we had had to burn four kitchen chairs and a small table looted from neighbours.

In spite of the voluptuousness of the banquet, which was well above average for our stringent times, Sally looked unhappy. But before I could suggest a mind-altering activity, such as Scrabble or a pillow-fight, to cheer us both a little, there was a sudden loud hammering on the door.

I sprang up, instantly ready to grovel, run, or gob – whatever was most socially appropriate. Sally grabbed my arm and pushed me into the cupboard under the stairs, stopping only to stuff the remaining cream crackers into my pocket. Then she shut the cupboard and opened the front door. I heard mens' voices; the front door closed, and several pairs of heavy boots thumped their way upstairs in a seigneurial, well-trodden kind of way. A door shut upstairs.

I waited for a while – enough time to discover that you cannot eat very many cream crackers unaccompanied by any liquid. Slumped against a redundant vacuum cleaner, spitting out crumbs, I pondered. Sally loves women, I've known that for years (although we've never discussed it, of course). Yet those booted chaps were up in her bedroom – clearly not here for a cup of tea and a slice of cake.

I decided to escape from the cupboard. To do this silently would be, of course, a triumph of muscular control and power – which lamentably I do not have. I knocked over the vacuum cleaner and trampled a few small crunchy items that hang round in dark cupboards. Luckily, whatever was going on upstairs was more interesting.

I began creeping up the stairs. Halfway up, I stopped. She was singing. With lazy passion, in her pure, full-bellied mezzo-soprano:

Sally free and easy,
That should be her name—

I, slightly less tunefully, whispered it along with her. In the patisserie of craziness, this surely took the biscuit.

Took a sailor's loving
For a nursery game.
All the loving that she gave to me,
Was not made of stone,
It was sweet and hollow,
Like the honeycomb.

After the singing came other sounds that needed no interpreting. How many men were up there? How often did this happen? And what the fuck were they doing to her? I wanted this to be over, but lacked the guts to go upstairs and, in sisterhood, add myself to this – what did punks used to call it? – 'squelch session'.

Preliminary departing noises suddenly smote my ear: coughing and shuffling and sounds of weapons being re-hoisted onto manly shoulders. So I scuttled back to my burrow until the boots had clattered down the path.

Sally was sitting in the kitchen; even in the candlelight I could see how tensely she held herself, dry-eyed and ghostly.

'You know what a vagina is?' she asked.

'I—'

'The word, you idiot. The meaning?'

'Er . . . Passage?'

'A *sheath*. Named centuries ago by some doctor. Some man. That's all it is, what we have. An empty scabbard, waiting for their pork swords.'

'Fuck 'em.'

She went to the cupboard she had eyed so lovingly before and took out a corked bottle. As she upended and drank, I could smell hospitals.

'They give you food, okay, and you let them fuck you, but why did you sing *so beautifully* to them, Sal?'

There was a long pause. She lowered the bottle.

'Ah, leave it,' I mumbled, hating myself for being the

witness to the dissolution of my friend. 'I'm going tomorrow.'

Her face closed then; a light went out, a curtain dropped.

'I have to wash. Do you want to come?'

We left the house clutching towels and walked in the harsh moonlight along the unnaturally lonely streets. By Battersea Bridge we stopped and climbed down to the shore. Sally gave me a pair of plimsolls to which I gave the only response possible with two fingers. She shrugged.

'There's broken glass here.'

She stripped, silently, efficiently, and began wading into the black water. After a while she began to swim. I watched from the bank.

'Don't dive in.'

I was still standing fully clothed at the water's edge. I had no intention of paddling, let alone diving.

'Sal, come out, you're turning grey-green.'

'It's not that bad. There are live fish in here. Don't swallow any water, though.'

Grimly, I removed my adhesive, unmentionable clothing. Maybe this was the purification I needed. Sally's voice rang out over the water, a liquid, plangent, essence of grief:

By the waters, by the waters, by the waters of Babylon,
We sat down and wept; and wept, for thee, Zion,
We remember, we remember, we remember thee, Zion.

I joined in the round as I slid myself into the cold and oily embrace of Old Mother Thames.

It was the strangest thing, singing into the emptiness of London with no one to hear us, no sounds of traffic our accompaniment. Standing waist-deep in the river in January and not feeling cold. The night sky wasn't burnt orange, as it always used to be, but navy blue, with a few anaemic stars challenging the bitter glare of the full moon; an unfriendly sky, heavy as the mud under my feet.

'He's dead,' she said in a matter of fact way.

'I don't think so.'

'If you find him – then what?'

'Haven't decided.'

'Liar!'

Then I experienced in a tactile way the jagged, pike-like things on the bottom, so I had to swim.

We started giggling, uncontrollably, swimming and trying to pull each other under, oblivious now of everything except the ridiculousness of dying by accidentally swallowing this ratty, faecal bilge.

'Life is a finite business,' says Sally later, when we lie, chaste and uneasy, on her double bed.

'Is that it? A business?'

She pinches my arm hard, and suddenly there is passion

in her voice. 'You know this ends, don't you? The food runs out. I give us a year, max.'

I can't think that far ahead. I have enough trouble differentiating past and present.

Suddenly she sits up in bed. 'Didn't they have the plague in Ireland?'

'It's global, isn't it?'

'Then how the fuck did you get here?'

I sing, as if it explains anything at all, '*Oh come, angel bands, bear me away on your snow white wings* – hey, do you think Guy is a Ref?'

I hear her sigh in the darkness. 'He's uninteresting.'

Hopefully, I seize on the lack of emotion in her voice. That's more like my pal. 'I'll find him. I think that's why I'm here.'

'Oh, I get it. Like *Les Jeux Sont Faits*. You've been resurrected to conclude your business with the lowlife you wasted five years of your life with.'

'Er – maybe.'

Her nursely hand reaches for my wrist, and after a few seconds, three fingers are pressed efficiently on my neck.

'You are not dead, whatever you may wish to pretend to me. You have a perfectly regular, strong pulse.' She thumps my chest. 'Can't you hear your heartbeat?'

I say lamely, 'Didn't Jesus have a heartbeat after he came back?'

She turns over and sighs. She's too tired to care. Gropes for my hand and squeezes. Hard to say whose hand is colder.

'I will find him, Sal. Even if all I do is kick the shit out of him.'

I get up to go to the bathroom and she says: 'Don't use the toilet. The rats crawl up and bite your fanny.'

So Oldie was right: you live and learn.

FOUR

EARLY NEXT MORNING I left Clapham and its enigmas and headed north. I was getting pissed off with urban life, to be honest, and now that I had drawn a blank on the Chestnut Avenue lead, I had nothing to go on but my instincts.

Around Walthamstow I struck lucky, finding a lorry half full of tinned food, guarded only by a few parped figures who seemed to be clenched in attitudes of frustration. It took me a while to work out why this should be, but after I had tried to open a few tins myself, I began to share, or empathise with, their body language.

Do you know how to open a tin of tomatoes without an

opener? Nor did I. Here are the fruits of my experience, for your future use, or, possibly, present amusement. First you look longingly at the label depicting juicy tomatoes for several minutes, occasionally swearing, then you pick up the tin and hurl it against the side of a lorry or similar hard object. When that doesn't work, you scrabble around for a bit of sharp stone and try hammering your way into the top. When that doesn't work, shouting abuse with all the power of your lungs, you jump up and down on it until – *Hallelujah!* you observe a small dent in the middle. Then you pick up the tin in both hands and work it backward and forwards, salivating at the juicy tomatoes you can now barely make out on the tromped-on label. Suddenly, the tin develops a small leak and you first of all nearly amputate both lips sucking greedily at the liquid, then, using good old human ingenuity, force the ignition key of the lorry which you have cleverly removed, into the small hole in the tin, and lever it open.

Then, hey presto, you empty the tomatoes into one cupped hand and slurp them up. Delicious.

While in mid-slurp it occurred to me that there might be some diesel left in the lorry. I could travel east and slightly north in style! I didn't know where I was going, but at least I could go there a bit faster. It's the kind of philosophy we all used to subscribe to in the old days, when the ultimate in frustration was being caught in a traffic jam watching the Nissan Micra you had nearly creamed yourself overtaking five miles back inching ahead of you in the slow lane, slowly, irrevocably, at a toddler's pace, fucking overtaking you in your BMW! Happy, uncomplicated days.

I climbed up into the cab, nervously swallowing, as driving is not, for me, one of the great thrills of life. Fragments of a tune rose to my lips as I began heaving the enormous parped driver, truly a magnificent monolith of a trucker, out onto the road: '*. . . the huntsman blew loud on his horn . . .*'—tried the horn, it responded like a moose-callers convention—'*. . . and all that he blew, it was lost and gone, was lo-ost and gone . . .*' I was quite far gone myself, high on the adrenalin of terror, by the time I had inserted my untidy frame into the driver's seat while he crumped, head-first, on the tarmac, looking just a touch sulky. '*Tarry a ho, sess-a, tirra la-la . . .*' I crooned, just to keep my spirits up, while twirling the key in the ignition and wondering what relationship this dashboard bore to the hippy-pink Morris Minor I used to drive three years ago.

Suddenly, with a mighty throb and lurch of full-throated basso profundo power, we were off!

How I wished I'd had someone to cheer me on my way.

Evening shadows were falling as Rodney finished his day's work. The little burden, trussed and lightweight in its black bin liner, had been gently consigned to the canal, where it sank in lazy, graceful zigzags to meet the others, each carefully weighted with bricks. He felt a pang of pleasurable loneliness as he turned and walked back along the footpath, a mellow, fulfilled melancholy, pregnant with the promise of another day.

The lorry and myself, locked in an ungainly pas de deux, are lolloping eastward and northward in a semicircular waltz, partly to avoid the occasional cars that loom up, as stationary vehicles do, with vicious abruptness, partly due to my inability to steer and change gear simultaneously, along what I imagine hopefully is the A12 dual carriageway. We have just passed the remains of an old holding camp; the wire fence is flapping around a concrete post, and a child's red dress, like a flag of surrender, flies gaily from the barbed wire. In the dusk I cannot see if anyone is there; in any case, they would be dead, of course.

Over to the east, where I guess Basildon to be, the sky is lit by orange and smudged with purple: firestorms. Other than that, there is no light except the magnificent choral blare of my own quadruplet headlights, scything their way through the charcoal grey night.

~

The babies were in bed; Clover and Amber were picking out P.J. Harvey songs from memory ('You mean, they've got memories, actually?' said Jamie) on the old upright piano in the playroom.

Gwyn and Jamie were crouching in the sweat lodge, naked and glistening in the candlelight. From the freshly cut, pliable young hazel poles of the bender, covered with many layers of tarpaulin and polythene, hung an asthmatic's nightmare of dusty dried herbs: bunches of sage, garlic, lavender and rosemary. Outside, hanging like votive offerings on the low branch of a young beech tree, fluttered towels and clothing. A fire burned in a shallow pit outside the bender, and deep in its orange heart, granite rocks were glowing.

A low murmur of voices and crackling footsteps stirred the men to activity. Swiftly they extinguished the megaspliff they had been sharing – Rose had a bit of a thing about being stoned in the lodge – and sprinkled a few drops of pine-scented water on the hot stones in the middle of the circle. The steam fizzed, and one of the rocks split with a soft crack. Gywn and Jamie shifted round to make space for the women who would soon be entering by the front door flap of the bender.

Stripping in the January night, their bodies blue-white in the barren light of the moon, Rose, Jerry and Lally hung their clothes on the handy branch of a rowan tree, then, shivering, approached the bender entrance.

Rose stooped and lifted the flap, saying in a low voice, 'All my relations.'

From inside the bender came a deep-voiced response: 'Ho.'

But everyone tried not to think about all their relations.

Silently, the women entered the lodge, shuffling their bare-bottomed way around the circle, gazing through the scented steam into each other's eyes.

Rose began crying immediately, and the others let her cry, staring stony-faced into the centre; last survivors of a stoic beleaguered tribe, or iron age cave dwellers suddenly returned to claim their newborn planet?

Silence.

Jamie felt incredibly relieved that he had spliffed up a bit with the biggie. These sweats were really getting out of order, emotionally.

Gwyn felt a savage surge of anger lubricating his throat and he spoke to the stones, in a furious whisper: 'Why? Come on, O great Spirit, why? Why all the babies? Why not me?'

Jerry made some ritual gestures, bowed her long neck with dignified sorrow, letting her curls tumble around her pale face, and made, as she always did, a graceful speech: 'We need to understand, O Spirit. We are not angry, we are in mourning: sad for the whole planet, sad for all the grieving and the pain and the dying. And we need to know, what must we do now?

Rose said, 'We celebrate the life of Rufus, whom we loved . . .' then subsided into more tears, flowing like elderflower wine. Jamie gently massaged her neck.

'Ho,' said Lally. 'Is that someone outside?'

They all tried to hear someone outside, but these days the question had to be rhetorical.

'We celebrate Bethan,' said Gwyn grimly, 'even though she wasn't a baby and this is supposed to be about babies, I can't help thinking about her, so . . .'

'Ho,' said everyone, remembering Bethan who had been the first to die.

'And Aslan. And Rainbow. And Chay and baby Zillah and Poppy . . .'

As the litany continued, Rose's tears stopped. She left the bender and dug a wide shovel into the fire, picking out the largest rocks, and dropping them, nearly red-hot, into the pit in the centre. Then she added more water until the temperature inside the lodge had everyone's eyes stinging with sweat.

'And for the ones who are left, O Spirit, what do you intend for us? Have we been chosen? For what?'

'Ho,' came the soft but heartfelt response, and Jerry, pleased with that rare moment of unanimity, hummed a Native American chant.

After a while Jerry took some sage and wild garlic and burnt it in a little pot, and while it was still smouldering, she passed it to each one in turn, ritually encircling them with the smoke that reminded Jamie of the roast pork and crackling with sage and onion stuffing that his mother used to make on Sundays—

'Now each share a thought,' said Jerry, fixing Jamie with her seer's eye.

'Er – me? Oh, I'm thinking about – er – being a child myself. My mother, and er'—God, he could murder now for a huge slice of pork and gravy—'wondering when I stopped being a child and I'm actually, you know, like, hungry.'

'Ho,' murmured everyone, and Gwyn pinched his thigh so hard he had a bruise next day, and Jamie felt like he'd farted in church. What was the matter with him? Weren't things serious enough yet?

'I'm thinking a terrible thought, O Spirit and everyone, and I don't want to share this, but I have to,' said Rose, and in the golden glow of the candle her face was the face of an angel. 'It's this: why did Rufus have to die, and not Kyra?'

In the shocked silence that followed, no one said 'ho'.

Somewhere in Essex the diesel gives out, but it is my bedtime anyway. I climb into a swelter of torrid duvet and pillows soft as a barmaid's thigh; tucked underneath which I find a lonesome trucker's dream enhancers – a big phallic vibrator-shaped torch, and a mysterious soft package. Vibrator flashing, wantonly expending my batteries, I investigate.

It is a customised present – Xmas wrapping paper with a back-slapping, blokey motif of dead herrings, tweed hats and grandfather clocks. A label with a childish inscription reads, 'To Uncle Gazza with love from little Jayden'. Greedily, yet with respect, I tear it open. It's a whole moist, fragrant ounce of Golden Virginia! I nuzzle it bestially for some minutes, unwilling to confront the unpalatable fact that there are no papers to go with it. Ah, Uncle Gazza, how could you do this to me! No papers!

Whimpering aloud in the darkness, desperate for some distraction, I open my rucksack and get out the dried seaweed. Munching on its salty potassium-and-iron-enriched fronds, I try not to fantasise what a perfect accompaniment a fag would be to this marine snack. Miserably, I glug down some water, and then haul out the mystery volume. It's 'Sense and Sensibility' – what extraordinary synchronicity! I open it at random, fingering the unsatisfactorily thick paper of its hardbacked pages, even rolling them a little as I consider a villainous violation . . . wouldn't Jane do the same, faced with this torment? I read morosely, unsmokingly, taking no joy from the measured cadences:

'*He was not an ill-disposed young man, unless to be cold-hearted and rather selfish is to be ill-disposed – but he was, in general, well respected; for he conducted himself with propriety in the discharge of his ordinary duties . . .*'

That's Guy to a T. And myself, in normal circumstances, I would find a sisterly affinity with the serene Elinor, who '*possessed a strength of understanding and coolness of judgment*'. But so fucking what? What would Elinor do, holed up in the cab of a lorry with no duties, nice etiquettes, or parochial callers to give life its subtle restraints?

Would Elinor – or even the sublime Jane – possibly have done as I now do, bellow obscenities to the unheeding night, doubled up with the bitterness of loss for a craziness I crazily miss, clutching the duvet as if it were my mother's skirts? Where do we go from here, with all our cool judgement and governable feelings?

I think about another missive, lying in wait in my

rucksack, but I can't read that, not tonight.

No, tonight is necrosed, it's a ball of bile I can't vomit up or swallow down. In this limbo, I seek the usual solace, flopped on my belly, my left hand snaking through the cleft of the Y fronts (must jettison them tomorrow; they've become ridiculous).

Like this, I should feel safe. Who could there be in the deep dark outside to harm me now? Who knows? Who's alive? Who cares? I'm wanking in the cab of a lorry, and what I say is, pants to the lot of you.

Guy was asleep and he dreamed that someone came and lifted him out of the bed, and in his dream he tried to protest, tried to explain that there was something under the pillow he must take with him, because they were a pair, a working partnership; and in the dream, a man with a young, smooth, unmarked face shook his hand, not meaning to hurt him, and promised to help him. Then he seemed to be in some kind of uncovered vehicle, moving bumpily with cushions of leather under him and he saw silhouettes of leafless trees gliding past against the ultramarine horizon.

The young man was talking, in a low serious monotone, thanking him; and there was a child in the story somewhere . . . and when the waves of pain hit him again, making him wonder if perhaps it wasn't a dream, there was a needle with a milky liquid that was slid into his arm, and a great pleasure welled within him, and he fell into its black caress with no sound.

In the morning he woke up, and he was in a different bed, so it wasn't a dream at all. There was a young woman sitting by the bed, and she smiled as his eyes locked open, astonished. Without a word she got up, and going to the door, called softly to someone. It was all so . . . old-fashioned.

The someone came in, and it was the same young man. He was wearing a grey suit and his fair hair was clean and cut in a professional, user-friendly style.

'I hope you'll forgive me,' he began, and there was no irony in his tone, 'but I don't want you to die. You see, once upon a time, you saved my son's life.'

A bottle came swimming into his field of vision.

'My name is Alastair. I'm sorry, we can't make tea at the moment. But it said in the *Daily Mail* that you liked whisky. It's a trifle early, I know – but I'll join you. Margaret doesn't drink.'

Guy remembered the needle. 'Are you a doctor?'

'Sort of. As good as, the way things are now.' Two crystal glasses were filled with a measure that was generous, but not unconventionally reckless. He shook his head.

'I can't. My fingers . . .'

'Those beastly . . . bastards.' It was the woman who spoke, and then guiltily pressed her hand to her mouth. 'Excuse me. It's just – they must have known who you were. They did – that – deliberately. Knowing it was the worst thing for you.'

'It doesn't matter now. Forget it, please.'

'Here.' Alastair held the glass to his lips as patiently as a mother, and he sipped, then gulped. Magic.

'Cheers. To – the future?' suggested Alastair, and the next minute his new guest had puked all over the candlewick bedspread.

~

Rodney is haunting the park with a discreet dark red silk carnation in his buttonhole, watching a little girl throwing bread to the ducks. At least, that is her game; there is no bread, so she takes handfuls of gravel from the path and throws them into the scummy pond, and the ducks play along.

'Where's your Mummy?' asks the stranger, and she points in the direction of a rhododendron bush. Then, with charming, unselfconscious urgency, she kneels down by the pond and spoons the filthy water into her mouth with a tiny cupped hand.

'Are you hungry?' He falls into step with her as she skips

back towards the bush, fingering the surprise in his pocket.

Rodney is used to sights, but this mother takes some beating; leaning against the trunk of the rhododendron bush, parped, of course, at least a week ago, with amoeba-like flesh deliquescing through the buttonholes of her blouse and her headscarf and face untidily gnawed away on one side; a jangling disharmony of green and irridescent indigo.

'Oh dear,' murmurs Rodney, wondering whether this is worth pursuing, 'Mummy's in a bit of a state, isn't she?'

The little girl tries to sit on the squashy lap, sliding and falling off and trying again, and a loving instinct makes him hold out his hand to her.

She is exotically beautiful; perhaps Persian, with thick sable lashes and a creamy-dusty skin that speaks of an indoor life spent in limousines and kelim-lined apartments. Her blue-black hair hangs in a long and ragged plait to her waist, clearly in need of her maid to restore its gloss with hours of patient brushing.

'This is for you.' He holds the biscuit just out of reach. 'Come with me, and you can have a whole packet just for yourself.'

She darts a loving look to the squelchy thing on the grass, and Rodney feels a bitter pang of jealousy, which he disguises admirably.

'We'll bring some back later for Mummy,' he promises, his face as soft and sad as yesterday's soufflé.

Breakfast, the morning after the unpleasantness in the sweat lodge, was eaten in unforgiving silence by the adults, their eyes avoiding Rose, who had spoken the unspeakable. Only the children giggled and argued over their creamy porridge and thick slices of toast and honey.

Rose kept looking at Kyra, who was eating methodically as always, frowning with concentration as she chewed, squinting along her spoon, suddenly and inexplicably flinging her arms wide, sending plates and bowls clattering.

Gwyn had Ross, his baby, on his lap, and rested one squat palm gently on his velvety skull.

In the corner of the room a walkie-talkie suddenly crackled and beeped into life, and Jamie picked it up. There was a brief business conversation.

'Payday,' he said after he put the machine down, 'George wants to know, are we going down to the Lodge or should he come up here?'

'What does he want this week?' Jerry tried to take an interest, but she couldn't understand why they needed George when they had so much spiritual power guarding them, circles and circles of it . . .

'He wants dope, honey, milk, eggs and bread.'

'He can't have bread, it takes hours grinding the corn and Amber and Clover didn't do their turn on the rota—'

Jamie tossed back his floppy hair; this was all so *lame*.

'If we don't give him what he asks for, he'll leave.'

'So?'

Gwyn said patiently, as he had said every time when this conversation came around: 'If he leaves, anyone can come in.'

'There isn't anyone out there! There's no one else left! Everyone's dead! Don't you get it yet?'

Lally threw an enamel plate across the kitchen and looked as if she would burst into tears.

'I'll go down and see him,' said Gwyn, standing up. 'Take Ross, will you, Lally?'

'Why don't you give him to me?' said Rose, and the silence grew cold.

~

It was touch and go whether I got up at all. Delicious warmth wrapped me all around, and distraction in magazine form was within easy reach: 'Girl meets Dog', 'Bondage Island', '101 Sexercises for Adult Males', 'Overcome your Shyness', and 'Growing Prize Roses The No-Mulch Method' were all mine for the taking. There was also a government booklet entitled 'Common Sense During The Epidemic', printed on cheap paper in a soothing shade of blue, which I, as a good citizen, read for at least a page before tearing it asunder, having ascertained experientially that it even failed the grade as toilet paper:

'Q: What if I develop flu-type symptoms?
A: Remain in bed until symptoms have cleared up.
Q: Is the immunisation effective?
A: If given in time, it is 100% effective.
Q: How can I best protect my family?
A: Do not listen to alarmist gossip. Do not succumb to panic. Eat fresh fruit and vegetables. Your doctor can help with mild tranquillisers.'

All this entertainment was mine, plus an abundance of tinned tomatoes, representing food and drink all in one handy package.

But yet here I was, scrambling down from my lovely nest, and squatting frankly at the side of the road, feeling unfulfilled and greedy for more thrills. I was on a journey. And what's the point of stopping anywhere nowadays? Besides, the Golden Virginia was burning a hole in my pocket.

I bade a client's farewell to my duvet, my counsellor, recipient of my nocturnal confidences, and, with a sudden access of noble savagery, I jettisoned all the books, the smug

A-Z, poor old Jane, whose only crimes were being too sensible and a little on the heavy side, and the shredded Government pamphlet, which would never have made even 50p on ebay. I bunged a few token tins into my pack – somehow the prospect of daily slurping more tomatoes failed to excite – and I was off, walking in the old, natural way down the middle of the A12. I felt that today might be lucky for me; maybe Capricorn was rising, or perhaps it was the spring-like weather, which was uncomfortably mild for January; I was soon sweating like a stoker under my coat, but too superstitious to hurl it into a hedge, remembering how I had come by it. Ere long I started singing, with no one to hear me but the birds:

'Through bushes and through briars,
I lately took my way,
All for to hear the small birds sing,
And the lambs to skip and play . . .'

The song tails away as something ahead on the road impinges on my visual consciousness. I approach it, but warily, simultaneously attracted by the glitter of new chrome in the sun, and repelled by the burnt-out blackness of the shape that seems to be tangled with it.

Here, proudly straddling the fast lane, lies a pedigree mountain bike, the labels still dangling from its saddle, the saddle still swaddled in its amniotic sac of green polythene;

chunky, deep-tread tyres, dynamo lights, springy luggage rack, a Minnie Mouse bell – in short, everything a travelling girl could desire . . . but.

Clamped to the handlebars are, of course, hands. A pair. Connected, though in the course of nature probably not for much longer, to a horizontal person, or ex-person, sporting a jaunty maroon and blue woolly hat-and-muffler set that might have been a Christmas present. Under the hat, a pair of neatly pecked-out eye sockets briefly give me pause, until, accepting their implicit challenge, I embrace the body; I tug. This isn't so bad; the easterly breeze carries away most of the smell, although underneath the imitation leather car-coat there is something going on – a moistness, a separation, a yielding – that makes my toes curl and sets the guts bubbling and heaving like fresh porridge.

The body shifts obligingly a few inches away from the saddle, but the hands, the vulturine talons, are still locked round the handlebars. I try kicking, at first gently, then with increasing violence until I accidentally uncover a wrist bone. Nothing moves. Tenacious, these bones.

I have a profound respect for hands, a respect particular to the few (very few, now) in our chosen profession; so I'm well aware of the twisted smirk on the face of Lady Luck, should she be beholding my dilemma. Unwillingly, I apply my naked fingers to a random digit, and am rewarded: the bruise-coloured flesh peels slackly away from the bone like overcooked chicken. Only nine more to go now, and while my squeamish eyes squinch shut, my mind sympathetically distracts by conjuring up an image: the fragile, bone-thin candles on my tenth birthday cake, in the shape of a circus tent with its jolly stripes of red, blue and yellow, the sudden searing pain of the melting wax splashing on my celebrant's thumb, the reflex vomiting re-icing the cake; my father's unforgiving, cold stare; the extinguishing of the kiddies' party spirit as effectively as a post-christening visit from the bad fairy . . .

Heroically, I make a grab for the bike's front wheel, eyes still shut, and begin a series of whirling, jerking, tugging movements. Something comes free and I open my eyes. The ex-person is now lying in a type of yoga pose, head twisted sideways, one arm flung across his body, one knee bent up; he looks cool. Apart from a few bony joints and knuckles still adhering to the handlebars, a stylish *memento mori*, the bike is mine.

I tuck my rucksack into the luggage rack and stand reflectively a moment, wishing for a more dignified mode or code of farewell to my athletic, carbonised opponent. There is none, except that the delicacy that has always been my trademark holds me back from rifling his pockets for papers, fags or matches. It's a little thing, but significant.

Then knuckles, bike and I, we set off.

For a while we make excellent progress, then, somewhere near the Essex-Suffolk border, a phenomenon occurs.

I see a figure cross the carriageway from the southbound side, vaulting over the barrier of the central reservation, to stand and face me. He flags me down.

As I heave to, I see he is wearing a policeman's uniform.

A myriad diverting thoughts flit like cartoon hummingbirds among the foliage of my mental landscape; the idea that he might really be a policeman definitely not one of this colourful flock.

'This your bike, is it, sir?' For answer, I both nod and shrug, affirmatively ambiguous.

'And where might you be going?' He's good, he's definitely been studying the form; he even has the regulation politely disbelieving cocked eyebrow; but I'm not fooled. I point in the direction of onwards.

'I'm afraid I'm going to have to ask you to come with me, sir.'

Before I can draw breath he has my elbow in a paralysing ju-jitsu hold, igniting a fresh flash of intuition that my first intuition was completely wrong. He really is a policeman. Together we negotiate the central barrier, myself one-handedly dragging the bicycle, like a reluctant spaniel, up and over. Together we approach the parked car on the soft shoulder. A police car!

I shake my thoughts about like an old duvet; so the Eppie was local, only a London thing – out here in the country we have law and order, society going about its normal merry business – the usual straight weirdo élite must be still in charge . . .

In a trice, he has me up against the side of the car, arms spread in pre-frisking posture, and there's no doubt about the authenticity, the professionalism of his approach; mental cogs and wheels and gears begin to grind and I find myself asking,

'Do you have any I.D.?'

Without relinquishing his hold on me, and not at all fazed by my husky, would-be androgynous tones, he reaches into his pocket and produces a laminated card which informs me that he is Sgt. Dennis Toller, Essex constabulary.

'It's a fair cop,' I find myself uttering, 'and what's the charge?'

'Conspiracy, arson, arseholes, incitement to rape, buggery and murder,' says Sgt. Toller, and starts giggling.

How I wish I was mentally alert in the mornings. If I had been, I might have registered and correctly processed some anomalies here more speedily; the white froth around Dennis's mouth, for instance, or the parped colleague in the front seat of the patrol car.

Slowly, I begin twisting out of his grip, escaping, but of course he's quicker off the mark than me; youth is on his side, plus all that expensive training, and he soon has my arm rolled behind my back, effortlessly squeezing and grinding together the small bones in my wrist, and we are moving to the bonnet of the car, and I am being bent over it, aware that something is going on behind me.

'Listen – Officer – Dennis – I'm not a Ref. I can show you—'

For answer, a meaty forearm is slammed down on the bonnet, sleeve pulled back, and for the first time, I see the tattoo; the letter R blackly outlined by the downward pointing triangle. Sgt. Toller is himself a Ref! (and a policeman? How has this happened?) and now he is happily succumbing to the lusty urgings of biology, for that is what Refs can do, given the opportunity, and he clearly sees me as one of those opportunities.

'FUCK!' I cry involuntarily, aware that it's not the most tactful expletive, and follow this up with some donkey kicks and a few suggestions as to where he could alternatively put it. In response, the twin pillars of his iron thighs tighten on either side of me, and he keel-hauls my arm a little further up my back, tugging in a businesslike fashion at the string of my obscene trouserings.

'Does it have to be this way? Sgt. Toller? Dennis?'

I let rip a series of puny farts, as terror and revelation strike both ends simultaneously. 'You're mad, that's it, isnt it?' I can't see his face, but I'm sure this makes as much sense to him as it does to me. 'Yes, you've gone mad watching your mates parping one by one and the fabric of society breaking down, haven't you, Dennis?'

'Completely wrong,' he says briskly, releasing my arm so that he can haul himself over me. Seizing his hair I attempt a reverse headbutt which he wilfully misinterprets as foreplay. He pinions both my hands in one of his, while the grimy Y-fronts, following police procedure, begin to slip their moorings. In a few moments we will be joined, flesh to greying flesh, and there's nothing I can do about it.

Sgt. Toller is all primed and ready to go, and he's going to go all the way, no question about that, but suddenly someone shoots him in the back, and I feel him wavering against me, still hard and willing, but less insistent, until his grip slackens and he falls away, away and down.

Slowly, gracelessly scooping up the flanges of my lower garments, I turn and bend over him. His mouth is opening and shutting silently and his skin tone has faded to a bluish, yet attractively translucent grey-pink, calling to mind a giant dead jellyfish I saw once on the beach at Southwold. I could reminisce; but clearly, as dying man, he has priority in the spoken word department. I watch his mouth for a while, for form's sake, although my prurient gaze is drawn, disgracefully, to his forlorn pink truncheon, adrift and startled, poking heavenward through the gap in his regulation blue serge trousers.

Even more slowly, I realise that whoever shot Sgt. Toller could at this moment be drawing a bead on me, and I begin to trundle for cover behind the patrol car.

Sgt. Toller rattles in a comfortable sort of way, like my old Morris Minor starting up on a frosty morning.

Another figure, relaxed and completely circular in shape, approaches unhurriedly, gun crooked on his elbow like a gamekeeper, and stands astride the moribund copper.

'You old ba-astard,' he says cheerfully, in the same East Anglian accent as the late sergeant, but not so posh, 'I got you, din't I? And you can come out, an' all,' he continues, gesturing towards me with the gun, and I do. I'm floating now, rudderless, in a rural sea which is infinitely more baffling than the placid urban millrace I so thoughtlessly quitted.

'Knoo him, I did,' my chatty new acquaintance begins, and I listen, I pay him attention, because this could be the last conversation I ever participate in.

'Was he really a policeman?'

'Yiss.' Rather ungraciously, he delivers to Sgt. Toller's

dead face a neat roundel of phlegm aimed at, and hitting, the hairy mole on his chin.

'And a Ref?'

'Yiss.' Not quite so friendly this time, he suddenly turns to me and, in the free and easy way that everyone seems destined to treat me today, he begins checking my inner arms. He is not pleased, and thrusts a bulge-veined bicep in my direction. Tattoo. He's another Ref. Two in one day – I must tell Sally, if I ever see her again.

'But – how—?'

'Prison, innit ? All Refs there, we was. Dennis too. He was a good con. Bad copper, though.' He eyes my belly, for some reason.

'You 'ad it, then?'

'Had? Sorry, I don't—'

'The shot. You still getting your monthlies, or not?'

So this is what we can expect now, in the small-talk department. Amazing how the biological imperatives have reduced – or is it refined? – us to this; pure animal. Except for our use of language. And tools. He's playfully aiming one of those tools at me as I shuffle my feet and try to look normally, socially, embarrassed.

'Sorry, I don't think we've been introduced, but no, I never had the shot. I'm as fertile as – well, you are, I suppose.'

He frowns thoughtfully. A pregnant, gun-loaded silence

falls, and I realise it's time to exert myself somewhat more energetically in the lifesaving department.

'Well, thank you, anyway. You saved my—'

'I saved your arse, didn't I?' He guffaws and I join him, tinkling with relief; we laugh like drains.

'Well, it's been great, but I have to—'

'Ooh noo you don't,'—the laughing stops and he thrusts out his lower lip petulantly; dear me, he is volatile—'you're coming along o' me.'

'Well, er – why?'

'Why? What kind of a stoopid question is that?' He spurns a few items with his huge foot: Sgt Toller's corpse, my bike, and a stray wing mirror.

'Hey. That's my bike.'

'No, it ent,' he says instantly, and I don't disagree. 'That over there. Now, that's a bike.'

Patiently, he hauls me back across the road and I sit pillion. He tucks the stock of the gun into his boot, introduces himself as Dave, and we're off.

Dave is essentially a ball of fat, with shoulder-length hair, three or four discrete stomachs, and a real leather jacket. He used to have a brother with a garage, hence the fuel for luxury use, if you can call potting policeman a luxury; more of a hobby, I suppose, and he did a bit of 'pooching' (took me a while to work that out), hence the gun. Apparently he has a harem, and I am to be one of them, because Dave has a mission.

'Re-populate. Single-handed. I want you all in the club before April. I got land, houses, everything. You can have a whole cottage just for you and the kids.'

Objections, tunnel-visioned, cowardly objections raise their little hydra heads. Hospitals, Caesareans, painkillers, midwives?

'I got a book on hoom birth, all that stuff. Good enough in my gran's day – she din't need no drugs. I'll do the deliveries. I love babies, kids.'

'What about how I feel? Suppose I don't want—'

'Listen, Linda, things is different now. We en't got time for dun't want, specially from the womenfolk. We just got to git on.'

I've been here before; here geographically, I mean, and heard this stoic East Anglian philosophy frequently expounded in pubs from Lowestoft to Long Melford. We're cut off from the rest of England here – no one passes through, they either stop here for life or pretend the Fens don't exist. Dave, like Oldie, has unexpectedly been given a little empire, divine rights, and a larger-than-life agenda.

'My name isn't Linda, by the way.'

'You look like a Linda to me. Any other objections?'

'Well – if you're planning to repopulate Suffolk and Essex

with hundreds of your kids—'

'Yiss?'

'Well . . . you're ugly. East Anglia will be teeming with ugly kids.'

He thinks about this for a while, and I wonder what's going on with my brain here. Do I truly want to self-destruct in this inconsequential manner?

Suddenly he ripples with laughter, and his stomachs roil and squirm together like mating hippos.

'Ugly! Yiss. We'll be the ugliest tribe in the whole of England!'

When the bike comes to a halt outside an old council house, he embraces me warmly before we go in – nothing oral, just a hug, but it betides ill. I believe Dave is absolutely a man of his word. Unfortunately for me.

'Woman!' he bellows, and a woman comes out of the kitchen. 'Get the women,' he continues, not very inventively, 'I want them to meet the new woman.'

She gives me a stony-faced sisterly glare of appraisal, and vanishes.

Dave squashes himself into a small armchair and kicks his boots off, stretching his legs towards an insubstantial twiggy fire in the grate. His feet are the worst thing I've smelt all day.

Slowly the room fills up with women. They perch on the

arms of chairs, on stools and pouffes; some sit on the floor. There are about thirteen of them, and they all have slate-grey eyes and stare slatily at me.

'This's Linda,' says Dave, clapping me on the back; standing solo on the floral carpet, I feel like Alice, growing, extending, neck telescoping, gazing down at the small-boned, pinched, joyless seraglio. 'Say hello.'

No one says a word. I eye Dave; his good humour washes over us, raggedly, like a North Sea surge.

'I snuffed old Toller today,' he goes on, 'just as he was puttin' it up Linda here. So now she's on her own, and I'd like for her to come and join us.'

'Look,' I say to a random pair of slaty, dead-end eyes, 'look, I didn't want to come here. Actually, I've got a – husband. I was on my way to find him.'

Dave, feet steaming, chuckles richly, and pinches my knee.

'Thass what they all say at fust, in't it, gals?' He slaps all the bums he can reach. 'Goo on, get in the kitchen, all of you. Hev a chat. Sort it out.'

The kitchen, which was lit in the old days by fluorescent strip light, has yellow and green wallpaper, turquoise fitted units, sixties-style metal chairs, and is even more cramped than the sitting room. By the light of a smelly paraffin lantern I find and sit down on one of the few chairs, and try looking some of them in the eye. Finally, I locate one who seems less flinty than the rest, and I address her.

'Do I have to stay?'

'We dun't want you,' says a thin, distant voice from the massed ranks.

'Well, can I go?'

''Tis not up to us.'

I stand up. 'I'm going. You lot can all stay here and get pregnant. I think you're mad.'

'Dave'll come after you.'

'I'm going to tell him you don't want me to stay.'

'Dun't you tell 'im that.'

But there's no conviction in it, and the tiny, flitting figures part for me like Red Sea waves as I make my lumbering exit back to the sitting room.

Dave is picking his nose and thoughtfully arranging the contents, for what purpose I do not like to conjecture, along the arm of his chair. His hair, I can now observe, is clagged with some unknown substance, which could be hair gel (unlikely) or some of his other bodily exudations. I feel suddenly pushed into the territory, not of Austen, but of Charles Dickens at his most extravagantly squalid.

'Dave, it's no good. The women don't like me.'

He raises his eyebrows. 'It's that Freda, in't it? She's the troublemaker—'

'No, Dave, it's me. I'd never belong here. They're all so small and . . . well, small. I feel like a man next to that lot.'

Dave suddenly eyeballs the bogeys, inquisitorial, frowning. 'Like a man, eh?'

Am I on to something here? Pursuing my advantage, I drop my voice a few more tones and throw my chest out.

'Yes. I lied. I don't have a husband. I'm not normal.'

Dave scratches, scrutinising me coldly. 'You're a woman, in't you?'

'Well – yes, but—'

'Goo ter heck with that stuff. You'll do.' He reaches towards my midriff and tweaks a stone of my – to me – entirely unappetising flesh between his hammy fingers. One hand snakes behind my buttocks, with fondling approbation.

'Lovely. Plenty there to keep me happy.'

Lost for words, I begin to laugh. Dave joins in, gusting like a Force Ten off Sole Bay.

'Thass more like it. Goo you in and get some dinner.'

So in I go.

The women accept my enforced presence with Fen stoicism. They feed me on baked beans and onions, then escort me upstairs.

What had been a row of council cottages had been painstakingly knocked through, transformed by the emperor Dave into a single long dormitory. Every woman has her own curtained off area, although, as they explain, they don't usually keep the curtains closed. Their nighties are neatly folded on the grey pillows. A woman called Brenda shows me an empty bed.

'This can be yourn. 'Tain't no-one's else's.'

I sit on the bed, clutching my rucksack to me like a boarding school teddy bear. The flock settles around me, detached but maybe slightly cheered by my obvious depression.

'I don't want to be Dave's concubine.'

Brenda lights a small hand-rolled fag; it smells like fishmeal or burning bones. 'E's not so bad. Better nor my last.'

'But I don't want anyone. I want to be on my own. I was quite happy on my own.' I begin to sound like a querulous eight year old. To my horror, one of them begins brushing my hair. Am I being adorned for the bridal bed?

'Is bark is worse nor 'is bite.'

'I don't give a fuck! Can't you understand? You're welcome to him. I want to go.'

There is a mild buzz of interest. I crank up the outrage in my voice.

'If he fucks me, it'll be rape. *RAPE!*'

Leaden silence descends, slow and inevitable as a theatre safety curtain. Tactfully they avert their eyes. Eventually one of them, staring at the threadbare carpet, frames a question: 'You dun't want to stay, then?'

'No! I fucking don't! Help me escape?'

But this is too sudden. They need time to digest. They don't do anything hastily, these Anglians.

~

Rodney did not eat lunch; his unusual, silky clothes are beginning to hang loosely on him. Perhaps he is starving to death; perhaps it's all part of his plan. The fact is that there are so many more interesting things to do besides eating. He is standing by his chest of drawers, now, gazing upon the bundles of banknotes, dollars and Swiss Francs; the breath comes faster in his thin chest, and his heart hiccups along in paces as precise and delicate as a thoroughbred Arab mare.

Next door, the little girl lies; she never spoke any words as such. Rodney suspects she couldn't understand a thing he said all through, which was a pity. Her skin is no longer creamy-dusty, but yellow as marzipan, and on her lower belly a small mouth smiles, revealing the little, scarlet secrets within.

He strokes the long, straight, blue-black hair that falls to his shoulders.

'Mummy's tired now . . .' he murmurs, feeling the comforting sensation of looseness and freedom below the tight suspender belt; stroking his silken thighs, a frisson of after-pleasure tenses his belly.

She had not liked the lipstick, or his clumsy attempts at singing a lullaby. There was such a lot of blood; and so much ugliness, so much screaming.

He thinks on the whole this one was ill-chosen. His eyelids are mauve and dreamy.

Rodney will wait till dusk, maybe till dark, when he will set off with the black bag on his shoulder. He has a feeling, an unease; there will be some fallout soon. His luck can't last. Maybe lie low for a couple of days, conserving energy, trying to find more Malvern water. Or maybe try further out, up to the North, away from the spacious parks and wide avenues of his London, his domain.

He closes the last drawer and stands up, smoothing down his dress. If it could only be like this for ever . . .

The word is that Dave is expecting me in his bower of free love tonight. He has his own room, mercifully distant from the dormitory. I attempt to elicit details of his endearing below-blanket quirks; but I forget where I am. This is Stonygroundsville, UK. Every slitty little mouth is snapped shut, every slaty eye is averted from my ingenuous questioning gaze. Brenda is the most loquacious: she says he's 'oonly normal.' In this context, my mind runs riot.

Darkness falls, in the way that everything happens here, with dismal predictability. Around nine o'clock we are served hot water in plastic mugs which the women call a nightcap.

'Look, you guys,'—I am beginning to feel as if I'm on pethidine now—'I have to get out of here, I mean I HAVE TO—'

'Everything be different tomorrow,' murmurs Freda, tucking her thin hair into a wispy net. I wonder how they can all be so unaffected by my plight, I wonder if I they are all on sedatives and if so, where are mine? My mind buzzes messily like a bluebottle at a windowpane, and I note with horror that the whole sorry bunch are climbing drearily into their nighties.

'By the way, who's pregnant?' I ask. For some reason, this causes a ripple of something small but indefinable amongst this tight-arsed group. 'Well?' I eye Betty, a melon-bosomed twenty-five year old. 'What about you? Are you?' She lowers her eyes, unable to lie. 'How many times has he put it up you, as he would say so charmingly himself?' Betty looks for help towards Freda, who simply purses her mouth tighter and shrugs, clutching her nighty to her skinny breasts. I seize on Marge, the oldest of the group: 'You must have had some children before? Are you in the club?'

'We dun't talk about suchlike things.' Marge says primly.

'He can't do it, can he? None of you's pregnant, are you? Who's infertile, him or you?'

'Shush,' says Brenda, 'he says he'll do it be April.'

'And what if he doesn't? Do you think he'll blame himself? Of course he won't. And he won't keep you alive if you don't do what he wants, will he? He'd think nothing of turning the gun on any of you.'

By now, all the grey little faces are turned in my direction; this is subversion – dangerous, hypnotic talk. I'm not even sure where this is going myself. I'm speeding on panic, flying blind. 'Why don't we all fuck off? Take his gun and go?'

Murmurs of disagreement hum faintly in my ears. Christ! They are like little tomb effigies, this lot, only not so endearing.

'Where does he keep the gun? Has he got more than one?'

A sudden bellow from the sultan's boudoir pre-empts any useful confidences.

'He wants his hot whisky,' someone informs me, 'then about half an hour after he'll be wanting you.'

'Why can't you put weedkiller in it or something?'

One of them actually takes my hand and pats it roughly. 'You still dun't get it, do you, Linda? This is no wuss than how it was before. We dun't mind. Do you dun't mind, neither. Better for all on us. We git by like this. Do you git by the same.'

I listen to this long speech with sinking heart. She's right. We will survive. Even this will pass. But the injustice of it strikes keenly. I've slept with men I didn't love. I've even woken up in bed with a few that I felt strongly I never wanted to see again. But never, in all my life, did I face the prospect of lifelong forced marriage and childbearing with someone so uncongenial. Maybe I'm being too dainty here; but as the song has it, *I'd rather die a maid, and be buried and in me grave . . .*

The countdown ticks by. None of the harem is allowed hot whisky, although I ask for it piteously. They offer me seconds of hot water, though, so I can see I am beginning to make inroads into their flinty little bosoms.

Finally the moment arrives. The bellow from below, from the lordly pavilion. I descend the narrow stairs with their bleats of encouragement fading behind me. I know what they're thinking. Just get the old rite of passage over, and she'll be right as rain.

Dave is draped in an orange velvet caftan-type garment which may once have been a loose cover for a three-seater sofa. By the romantic light of a small paraffin lamp he looks quite sultry, in a sumo wrestling kind of way. He beckons me to him with a fat forefinger. I hang back by the door.

'Where's the gun?'

'You what?'

'Your gun. Is it in here?' He looks about him, puzzled.

'I want the gun in the bed with us.' Now he looks definitely startled. 'It's a kind of kink I have. It excites me.'

Intellect working overtime, he studies me thoughtfully. 'Are you taking the piss?'

'Dave – straight up. Guns turn me on. Would I mess with you? That wouldn't be very clever, would it?'

'Thass enough stoopid talk, get in the bed.' He breathes whisky towards me – it smells quite festive, Christmassy. Coyly I edge towards the bed, still fully clothed. He grips my wrist and pulls me off-balance towards him, his hand fumbling into my coat.

'Git this old bugger off.' I get out of the coat, awkwardly negotiating his grip on my wrist. He tugs at my shirt.

'Why din't you get undressed afore?' Complacently he pats the caftan somewhere in the lower ranges of his stomachs. 'Wanter see what I got?'

'I, er, think I can guess, actually.' Leering into my startled eyes like a stripper, he begins popping the velcro down the caftan front, and I fill in with appropriate mental music for him, meanwhile taking off as few clothes as possible as slowly as possible. Then his enormous arms pull me into the softness of pillows, feather mattress, duvet, squashy flesh, all melding and moulding together, and as I struggle for breath the flickering light from the lamp reveals Dave's equipment to be as ponderous as a bull elephant's rig, swinging in slow motion beneath his series of stomachs; the whole somehow impressive, in an awful way. Dave flips me onto my side, breathing heavily. He inches his massive endowments gruntingly towards me, contriving to roll a few stomachs beneath him until he actually takes on a reasonably normal, plump shape.

'Oopen up, gel.' And a playful pinch on my inner thigh establishes the beginning and end of official foreplay as the point of no return begins to nudge my unwelcoming crevice; then something happens. Before I know what I'm doing, I have seized a pair of testicles the size of tennis balls, one in each hand, and twisted them, fiercely with all my strength, in opposite directions. My hands, when roused, are as strong and wiry as the next man's, and now they operate like things possessed, screwing and turning until Dave, his eyes popping, bawls a mighty 'aaargh' of pain and surprise, and, suddenly remembering a self-defence class I once went to, I begin bellowing too: cries of '*Fire!*' (which apparently gets a better response than 'Rape'), alternating with wordless, howls that chime in disgraceful harmony with Dave's bullish basses.

Just as his arms are flailing in my direction, and it can

only be a matter of time before he wreaks his revenge, the bedroom door is flung open and a gathering of little greyly dressing-gowned figures stand there, gawping. At least, any normal people would have been gawping; they merely open their lips a fraction.

'I think he's having a heart attack!' I shout ingeniously, and about five of them come closer. By now, Dave's face is as purple and shiny as a bursting grape and although he would like to kill me, he can't think of anything except the pain. Under the covers, my hands retain their lunatic grip, while the rest of me squiggles as far away as I can.

'Come out the bed,' suggests Brenda.

'Yes, I'd like that, very much.' I give a final wrench, and a few punches in the area of the whole equipment before backing out of the bed with my honour intact. I grab whatever clothes I can, and leave the room. I hear him gasp, 'She's killed me!' as I stumble back up the stairs into the dormitory, brushing aside the mothy, questioning figures that seek to detain me, grabbing my pack, hurtling myself down the stairs and into the sweet night air, pulling on trousers, boots and coat. Then I duck back into the sitting room, and with a supreme stroke of luck, locate the gun. I loose off a round at the walls, and upstairs I can hear cries of something – not outrage, exactly, more pipsqueaking disapproval. Shouting with all the power of my lungs, I give them my finale: 'I've got the gun – don't try and follow me – I'm mad anyway – sisters, you could do this – throw off your shackles – I'm out of here . . .'

As I stumble blindly down the garden I collide with a cranky old bicycle, and drag it from the brambles it was overgrown with to the road. Creakily pedalling along on two flat tyres, I wait until the sobbing breaths quieten in my chest until giving voice, with moderate volume, to a triumphant verse of 'Jerusalem'.

After about a mile I fling the gun in a deep ditch, and hear it sink with even deeper satisfaction. I pedal along the incompetently signposted Suffolk lanes, turning left whenever I reach a crossroads. I hope by this method to be heading generally north and east – but for now, all I wanted was to be away from the unspeakable Dave and his cheerless concubinage.

Fear, excitement and adrenalin give me the energy to go on cycling until the first orange streaks of dawn begin to show in the easterly sky, when I realise I have been pedalling due west – but no matter. I am free. I am knackered, but free.

FIVE

FOR LUNCH, Rose has made leek and potato soup with cream, brussels sprouts with pickled walnuts, and sweet, fresh wholemeal bread. This is her way of apologising.

Jamie has been playing Finn's guitar all morning, wishing Finn was still alive to hear the fabulous new riff he's invented.

Clover and Amber, bored with reading Marie Claire for the fifteenth time, have been helping Kyra in the guinea pig house.

Jerry and Lally have started a Tai Chi class for the babies; Ross is just learning to crawl. Holly is five and has begun to read. Carly, her sister, is three and doesn't talk since her parents died.

Gwyn has been to see George at the lodge gate, sorted out his payments, and then ridden round the perimeter wall, checking for gaps. He also took some time to visit Bethan's grave. He carved most of the headstones, but he still can't quite believe that people he knows are buried under them.

Amber is scared to tell anyone she has toothache.

At lunchtime the walkie-talkie crackles again. Rose picks it up.

'George says there's a man at the gate. Sort of a tramp. He's asking, can he come in?'

'Find out a bit more first.'

'George says he's a dirty old boy but he speaks posh.'

'How old?'

'Says he can't tell.'

Gwyn said, 'What can he do for us?'

⁓

'They want to know, what can you do for them?'

'Er – news from London?'

Inscrutably, he passes this on.

'They say they dun't want to know nothin' about London.'

'Storytelling? Entertaining the kiddies? I used to be able to make great meringues.'

He repeats tonelessly, ‘Says ’e can make meringues. Storytellin’. Kiddies’ parties.’

A sterile pause. ‘Anythin’ else?’

With a rare flash of foresight, understanding the importance of getting in, I play my trump card.

‘I’ve got an ounce of Golden Virginia.’

Long, complex silence, followed by a guinea-pig-like chittering on the walkie-talkie. The sentry eyes my pack with an unpleasant smile on his graveyard features. The unknowns are disputing, clearly.

‘Well – do they smoke or don’t they?’

He laughs sourly.

‘Look – oh, fuck it, I don’t want food, all I want is some water and a bit of help with the map.’

He passes this on and waits for the reply, chewing his lip. Then he opens the gate, lowering his rifle to do so.

‘Go on up the drive, ‘bout half a mile. Big house. Can’t miss it.’

‘Thanks,’ I say. ‘Do you mind telling me who they are?’

He pauses, thinks, rolling his eyes. Looks at me: sifting, categorising, pigeonholing. ‘Hippies.’

‘Hippies? What, you mean like, 1970s hippies from Glastonbury?’

He doesn’t alter a facial muscle of his inscrutably Suffolk expression. ‘Everyone calls ‘em the hippies. Always has.’

'Oh, great. Thanks . . .' I wave ironically, walking backwards away from him, but he's already deleted me, and turned back to the Lodge Cottage, to whatever pastimes his lonely existence affords.

I enter a big kitchen with a stone floor and immense refectory table round which these hippies are sitting. I drop my pack and shift about, diffidently, feeling the weight of many pairs of eyes. Then one, the beautiful pre-Raphaelite one with reddish hair, gets up and comes towards me.

'You're a girl! George got it all wrong. Typical George!'

She's an immigrant to these parts; the taint of North London is in the whine and languor of her voice.

'More of a woman, really,' I offer, my recent encounter with Dave too fresh in my mind for comfort. I don't want to start off on the wrong foot. Despite my youthful appearance I am old; compared to this lot, very old.

I don't want warmth, intimacy, family life, sharing of confidences, relationships. I reject all the elements that combine to make these beautiful people the way they are – ageless, childlike, emotionally honest, financially untroubled – all that shit.

'I'm Rose.' Her long thin clean fingers clasp my hand. She introduces me to everyone. I forget all their names immediately.

'Now. Tell us about you.'

'Look – I got a bit lost, I'm not great at navigating. All I need is to fill my water bottle and get my bearings. Then I'll be off.'

For answer, one of them, the gangling, boyish musician-type with the irritating pale brown floppy hair and the torn-at-knee jeans and crumpled but clean white shirt, brings me a bowl of fragrant, creamy soup and a warm, soft crust of bread spread with butter. Another one, with a pale face of sculpted marble, tumbled natural curls and fabulous eyelashes, beckons me to the table and hands me a spoon.

They all gaze at me with eyes as gentle and curious as a herd of tame gazelles, smiling enlightened smiles. I am their day's good turn, obviously.

I dribble. I eat. I smile back. I can't help it. I'm suffering from a biological urge, same as the Refs.

~

In a high white tower there is a round room, and round the table there is a meeting in progress.

'. . . peaked, I should say, obviously still one or two minor pockets, but basically, all over bar the shouting . . .'

Speaker smooths the twin locks of hair stickily over his nude scalp, smiling, pleased with the effect. He has missed a third lock which trails, bending the wrong way, over his collar.

'. . . possible exception of the North . . .'

'. . . under a million, are we talking now?'

'. . . no statistics yet . . . fewer, probably.'

'. . . no more worries about climate change then, ha ha . . .'

'. . . nor peak oil, ha ha ha!'

'So.' Speaker drinks from a plastic mug, loosening his collar as he rubs his neck. 'We're in agreement, I don't think there's much doubt about that? Hm?'

'Vote on it?'

'Vote to vote on it? Carried.'

'And . . . carried.'

'Stage One . . . mm . . . Brigadier Jeffryes?'

'. . . or as we should perhaps say now, Sir Geoffrey?'

'Stage One is over. Stage One was Disintegration.'

'And Stage Two, Sir Geoffrey?'

'Selection.'

Guy has slept for a day and a night, and Alastair has given him vitamin shots. Also iron, potassium, high-protein plasma, and something that brings him effortless, dreamless, painless sleep.

Alastair never seems to sleep, and Margaret sits in Guy's room, knitting, bringing him water, opening and closing curtains, and sometimes offering him peculiar, ill-chosen meals: pickled beetroot, pilchards and chocolate wafer biscuits, for example. He knows what their problem is, and if he was well enough to leave, he'd go . . . but they say they want him.

'You're not out of the woods yet,' is the kind of cheerful thing Alastair says each morning, after he's taken the temperature and the pulse and looked at the eyelids, 'but you've been reprieved. A remission. Or a stabilising. Don't let's worry about the technicalities.' He smiles a Hackney G.P's distant, gone-fishing smile and then, refocusing, gently inspects the bandaged hands.

'They can come off in two days. I'm very optimistic about your right hand, that's good news, isn't it? Not so sure about the left, the bones were pretty far gone . . . maybe a little mobility, maybe not.'

Alastair used to be a vet. This is why he was in the hospital, searching – the word pillaging is hardly appropriate for a man like Alastair – for any leftover medical supplies, to be used humanely, without asking anything in return, to help survivors of the Eppie. Alastair is methodical, optimistic, but reasonable. He is using a mixture of medicines, some human, some animal, but, as he always points out, 'There's nothing here I haven't tried on myself. And what have we got to lose?'

Margaret always chimes in then with, 'Circumstances alter cases.'

They show him a picture, a recent photograph, of a little boy.

'That's Greg. On his fourth birthday. He thought the world of you.'

Greg's dead now, of course; but this doesn't affect the respect they have for Guy, or Desmond – they sometimes confuse the names.

Every morning he and Alastair take whisky together. It makes him feel sick, but to say so would be churlish.

He is not left alone much, and when he is, thinks fleetingly about Billie; feels sure she is dead. He thinks about dying. He thinks about mistakes, wrong decisions he made, and that question we all ask ourselves – what the fuck am I *for?* None of this does he share with his hosts.

Soon, when his hand is better, soon he will start talking. Prattling. Chattering. Soon, they won't be able to shut him up.

⸻

Kyra is kindly showing me the guinea pigs. There are fifteen. They live in a house. Yes, they have a real cottage, all to themselves.

'Upstairs is for rabbits,' says Kyra, 'and stick insects. And we will have the doves, the doves will come. And Holly . . .' She stops, mouth open, staring at nothing. Her tongue writhes, her lips move all on their own. Then she comes back. 'Holly's cat going to have kittens. Five kittens.'

'What about rats?'

Her body startles at the idea. She eyes me unblinkingly. 'I never want the rats.'

'Rats make lovely pets.'

Then she makes it into a joke, and she smacks me in the midriff, crowing and rocking her head from side to side, 'Rat's not a pet! Gwyn will shoot the rats, he will shoot them.'

This cottage in the grounds of the big house was where Gwyn and Bethan and Ross lived before. I try not to look at the druidic, emotional, bohemian outflow, the notes and drawings and photos blu-tacked everywhere, the Celtic odes chalked on the kitchen walls, the evidence of passion – fertile, messy; it somehow diminishes Gwyn, for whom I already feel respect. I don't want to know how deep his pain is, how intense the loss.

Kyra and I sit in two armchairs, stroking sandy shorthaired guinea pigs.

'How did you get your name?'

'I gave it to me. I chose Kyra.' Her mouth flaps open and shut, and she tries out a word. 'Vera.'

'What about Vera?'

'Was my name.'—minimal shaking of her head, so her lank, dead straight hair falls in her eyes—'not Vera. Kyra now.'

She gets up and walks to me and dumps the guinea pig in my lap and stabs my chest with her forefinger.

'You.'

'Me?'

'Name. Your name.'

'Billie.'

'That's for a boy!'

'It's a girl's name too. A woman's. Mine.'

'Okay.'

'Okay.'

Gwyn comes in, as polite and hesitant as if this wasn't his house. There are dreams here, his and Bethan's, and he's trying not to tread on them.

'Want to come for a walk? I'll show you our King.'

He's serious, it seems, so I had better be too.

He's carrying Ross, his baby, comfortably looped over one forearm, the baby's cheeks slightly puffed out with comic resignation. For the first time, I catch that baby's eye, and he transmits to me in the way of babies – uncanny, wise, nakedly eternal – a wordless message, which could best be translated by a series of question marks alternating with exclamation marks. His face lights up with a smile that I like to think I have inspired.

All around the perimeter is a high wall, topped with two rows of barbed wire. I give Gywn ten out of ten for energy, even if this anti-vandal stuff seems a little excessive, Suffolk not being generally famous for its levels of domestic crime. But he thinks ahead, and there were some rolls of barbed wire to use up, and the result is as good as a motte and bailey.

'I check this every day, and we have George guarding the gatehouse.' But he makes a wretched face; he is seeing something I can't. 'We could last for years here. We have our own well. We save seed, we can farm, cook, garden; we use what resources we have. Unlike some.'

Does he mean me? The urban butterfly that has, so far, not brought anything to the table except thumbnail sketches of some small patches of London, and an ounce of tobacco?

'Here.'

We've stopped. Looking up, a canopy of oak leaves, green, yellow, russet brown. The trunk is enormous. Before I have time to back away, he gently places Ross in my arms, and before I have time to hand him back, he vaults into the lower branches of the tree, and sits there, gripping the branch and swinging his legs.

Ross is used to inadvertent intimacy with strangers, and he copes with it a lot better than I do. I've never held a real baby. Puppets, of course, we had, and quite realistic ones, but the mystery of how that tiny body holds together and does not droop elastically from my grasp like a piece of human chewing gum terrifies me, keeps me vigilant. He is smiling, dreamy. I turn myself so he can look towards the tree, where his father is standing upright on the massive limb now, looking as if he wants to climb higher.

'How old is this one?'

'Five hundred years, four hundred – he is the king of them all.'

Briefly I toy with the idea that he is a genuine tree worshipper, a real Welsh Druid – but where's his beard?

'Do you play the harp at all?' I find myself asking. He shakes his head, unsmiling; he's miles away.

Ross's face puckers in slow motion, and with a tiny bleat of distress he reaches his arms towards Gwyn, who is back with us in an instant.

'How old is he?'

'Eight months. Just old enough to remember his Mam, I hope.'

I feel a perverse sense of loss now that warm bundle is no longer weighing me down, no longer smiling at me or needing me, just gazing at Gwyn with utter, all-embracing love.

Gwyn bends his head and softly brushes his lips against Ross's head, where the dark hair grows, fuzzy and infinitely soft.

'Let's go back. Everyone's cheered up since you came. And – we're going to need you soon.'

Ah, not a Druid then, but a Seer, a Prophet. It's a cheerless existence when everyone else is a hedonist with the attention span of a mayfly. Or maybe I do them all an injustice. While we're out here being slightly poetic, others are inside creating exquisite dinners. Be humble, girl. Nod and don't, whatever you do, start giggling.

'She's ten,' said Rose, when we were washing up after supper, 'and she's very bright. We did a lot of Steiner stuff with her, you know?'

I didn't. Children are a closed book to me, apart from once being my faithful customers.

'I think she'll read, eventually. Down's Syndrome kids have a lot more potential than people think . . .' (But she sounds as if she's going to cry at any minute.) 'Jamie's very patient with her. He's teaching her the tin whistle.'

The water comes from a pure and bottomless well supplying the house and the everlastingly alight and heartwarming Rayburn range. The kitchen is lit with artistically placed paraffin lamps. Yes, I'm living in a movie. Romantic comedy? Existential tragedy? Oh, shut up and talk to this nice woman.

'She decided to change her name, she told me.'

'Rainbow – one of the big girls – teases – used to tease her . . . said we got her name off a bottle of shampoo. Vera – you know, aloe vera. They used to say 'Allo, Vera' all the time. When she was, oh, I can't remember, six, she re-named herself. She's always been like that. A survivor. Jerry sorted out a little ritual for her, a naming ceremony. It was beautiful.'

Tonight I am to have a real bath, and Jerry will drop in some essential oils: lavender, juniper and cypress (to prevent varicose veins).

In half a day these hippies have charmed nearly everything from me: my life story (selected extracts, with no regard for consistency of tenses or chronology of events), my previous profession, my five years tethered to Suffolk seasides. Of course they never had a telly darkening their doors, because you can't be part of the alternative society while still pulling on the milkless dugs of the old mainstream one, but Jerry thinks she remembers visiting Southwold beach once, vaguely recalls two costumed figures frantically capering in front of their fairground booth, puppets on both hands, shouting to the salty air. Our childrens' show, 'Desmond and Lola' was, we fondly hoped, somewhat subversive; a new take on Punch and Judy, with schoolboy Des in charge of sleazy Lola's squalling brat and various incoherent plot twists, changed by us from day to day to pre-empt our precocious audience from shouting out the punchlines to our (very old) jokes. We foolishly considered it kept us sprightly, gainfully employed and functioning as a duo – and it brought in the pennies.

Not having a telly, they have never seen Desmond in his new incarnation, as the star of his own one man show – one man apart, that was, from Big Dez, his necessary but unfunny sidekick. Everybody needs a helping hand, and Guy's was right up inside his protégé, voicing his nasty schoolboy innuendos – oh dear, it sounds as if I used to while away my unemployed hours watching it myself, noting the gags I had written being plagiarised and cheapened for the BBC dollar. I don't tell them this. I have my dignity. I have had a life, of sorts, after puppets.

Their trust breeds, it is fungus-like; I can feel myself softening, liquefying, my whole being a knotted muscle kneaded to putty by a masseur's hands. Later on I'll be having one of those too, from Lally, while Jerry does a Tarot reading for me.

'Billie?'

'Yeah?' I am trying to balance two Le Creuset pots on the edge of the Rayburn to dry them.

'I'm really glad you came. I think – I think It Was Meant.'

In the old days, pre-Eppie, I'd have cracked up laughing at

this point; beautiful as Rose is, lovely and mellifluous as her voice is, I recognise only her fluency in New Age tosh . . . but things are not the same in this decimated world. Signs and signals are all we have now. I nod wisely, empathically.

Rose dries her hands, shooting me a glance I can't interpret.

'We were having a bad time . . .' She breaks off. 'Do you want a smoke?'

She said a smoke. This is not a straight fag I'm being offered. It's got to be home-grown, praise be.

In no time she and I are sitting at the table rolling a genuine fatty – a tobacco & home-grown spliff, bursting at the seams with dreamtime goodness. I refrain from commenting how like the old days this is, because Rose has a sob in her breath, and her hands are shaking, and here it comes—

'You see, Jamie and I, we – we had another child, younger than Kyra. He was perfect. He was beautiful. His name was Rufus.'

From the West, they are coming now. Travelling by day, by night, capriciously as the mood takes them, arguing, jostling, fucking, screaming, wasting, tearing doors off houses and branches off live trees to make their fires, setting their dogs to attack sheep, cows, rabbits, any meat they can eat; their kids are a hungry vicious flock who lie and cheat and steal and kill. Travelling along the old roads in convoys a mile long, abandoning the cars as they run out of fuel, abandoning the kids, the pregnant slits and bitches, the losers who can't keep up. They aren't predictable, this bunch; they aren't green or kind or fair. Spewed out from the swirling, random malice of cities, they are voracious, and the naked, barren land is their prey, their sacrifice.

They have no leader . . . and his name is Mart. Smarty Marty. And he rides a black horse that no one else can ride, and as they move across from Swansea to Bristol to Birmingham to Luton to Norwich, a spinning, dizzy ball of noxious gases, they attract, they magnetise, they pull the surviving world into their field of gravity.

'The wall has a weak point down by the road, it needs mortar and I'll do it tomorrow,' said Gwyn that night, as we sat around the fire. I was, to be honest, half-asleep; post-bath, post-massage, post-smoke, I lay back against Jerry as she rubbed my hair with a towel, scarcely breathing. The Y-fronts have been composted, the bagman's outfit is to be recycled for Rose's scarecrow, and tomorrow I will be dressed in some of Finn's clothes – he being the only person of my size and build – so that instead of looking like a tramp, I shall look like a suave hippy tramp.

'Don't give yourself any hassle about it, man,' reproaches Jamie, accompanying his words with a plaintive guitar riff.

Gwyn explodes, extra-Welsh: 'You don't get it, do you? You still think we're living in the old world, the liberal do-nothing world.'

Jamie's mouth drops open in protest. 'Chill out, man, I was the one that found the prophecy.' He nods at me: 'You know Nostradamus?'

'Not personally.'

' "A scythe joined with a pond in Sagittarius" – you know the one I mean?'

'Refresh my memory.' I've often observed that the first sense to go when stoned is awareness of subtle humour.

'Plague, famine, death from military hands; the century approaches its renewal.' Jamie nods, smugly. Gwyn explodes again.

'So that's that, is it? It is written – so you sit back now and let it happen. You bloody astrologers are so fatalistic that apathy becomes a bloody philosophical straitjacket in the end.'

Everyone is too stoned or correctly diagnosed as apathetic to argue.

To my surprise, Gwyn indicates me. 'She can tell you. She's

come from the real world. Tell them what's happening – go on, tell them, Billie.'

I struggle to a more vertical level, re-assembling my grasp of language.

'Er, well, the century has actually been renewed for quite a few years now. Oh, and this morning I was nearly raped by a mad policeman on the A12.'

'There you are. Nothing's changed.' Jamie, smiling wearily, infuriatingly, slides a bottle down the softly screaming strings of his guitar, shaking his hair back from his face.

'The only thing that's different,' says pink-faced Lally, in her little-girl's voice, 'is that there's hardly any people any more.'

'Yes,' Gwyn hisses, lifting himself out of his chair with the force of his own volubility, 'yes, but that doesn't mean we won't ever be meeting any of them. And that doesn't mean that when we meet them, they're going to be nice. It isn't only nice people that survived.'

I agree, but with less energy and passion.

'There's a man called Dave living less than five miles from here in a council house who's kidnapped thirteen women and he's planning to impregnate them to swamp East Anglia with his ugly descendants.'

'Holy shit,' says Jerry, dreamily, 'shall I roll another one?'

Later, we started singing. Now they knew I was a performer, of sorts, they pressed me to sing, and after Gwyn had sung a Welsh song, in Welsh of course, in a huge baritone way and Jamie and Rose had played 'Can't Buy Me Love' on guitar and whistle, and Lally had sung very softly about ' *. . . earth, air, fire and waters, we are the mothers and the daughters . . .*' I picked up the whistle, remembering a merry night in Galway a few days before I started sneezing – it must have been the night I ate my last sausage.

'Do you know this one?' I played 'Star of the County Down' in the way that English people play Irish music, and there was a kindly, reverent silence; when I finished they pressed me to do some more, and some uncanny spirit took possession of me, and before I could stop myself I was singing that ancient, bitter song from the Irish – the weirdest and most potent of chants for the dead:

> *'I am stretched on your grave and would lie there forever,*
> *If your hand was in mine, I'd be sure we'd not sever;*
> *My apple tree, my brightness,*
> *It's time we were together;*
> *For I smell of the earth, and am worn by the weather . . .'*

Oops. Bad choice there, girl. Hurts, desires, yes, and sudden, prescient stabs of loss, all came clawing and raking at my throat; a turbid, poignant lava of molten sentiment threatening to overspill, to disgorge its poisonous cargo. But, in case of emergency, break glass with hammer. All I needed to do to make it all go away was breathe. Hard.

'It's okay,' Gwyn suddenly whispered, and I could hear the tears in his voice as he touched the back of my neck with a hand as warm as a fresh-baked doughnut, 'let it go.'

Immediately, they clustered round, trying to hug me, most of them in tears, some offering clean linen handkerchiefs, all suggesting that I let it go, let it all go . . .

Let it go? That isn't how I got where I am today. Letting go is for softies. I see myself suddenly, from above: detached, contained, alone. Delightfully and comfortably alone.

'I don't do crying.'

Rose laid her cool hand on my hot and oily forehead, beneath which what remained of my brain was spinning with dope-enhanced clairvoyance.

'You know what, Billie? You belong here.' She smiled through her bleary tears and even with a shining, ruby nose she still looked exquisite, a Raphaelite angel.

After the songs, it seemed to be bedtime, and some of them went up the big carved staircase, swinging lanterns and carrying hand-made candles and I saw who seemed to sleep together: Rose and Jamie, the lucky surviving couple, and Lally and Jerry, which left just the two of us sitting by the dying fire.

Gwyn pours me elderflower tea and I hope he won't talk about his dead wife. Or ask me what I am thinking.

'What are you thinking?'

'About a bike I found yesterday. Beautiful brand-new mountain bike and I—'

Gwyn pokes the fire adroitly, suppressing something – curiosity, anger, lust?

'Why can't you be honest? You haven't really told us anything, have you? Where are you going? What are you looking for?'

'Did I say I was looking for anything?' He gives me a look which says, as clearly as words, that I'm insulting his intelligence. 'Okay – maybe I am. But only out of misguided curiosity and a need to gloat over someone else's misfortune.'

'It's important to you.'

He's sitting, or crouching, too far away to touch me, but I can feel his spirited energies wriggling towards me like an upended basket of frisky young cobras.

'I wouldn't say important. It passes the time. He may be dead. Probably is. I hope so.'

Now he slithers down from the sofa to hunker next to me on my cushion. He fixes me with his supernaturally large eyes.

'I adore Bethan. I can't say adored, even though—'

'Gywn – don't—'

'—she's been dead less than a month.'

'About that song . . . I shouldn't have . . .'

'Don't be sorry. It helped us – helped me. It's powerful, isn't it, that song . . . and she, she must be so . . . lonely, out there in the field.'

He buries his square, dark, boxer's face in his hands, rubbing the bluish whiskered chin so hard it turns white.

'Do you hear what I'm saying?' His voice is muffled, distorted by his fingers.

'Well, I don't, really—'

With a blare, an eisteddfod of rage, he kicks the cosy chintzy sofa away, and I collapse loosely, spinelessly backward and he grips my hands and pulls me upright, standing, staring face to face – strange, I thought I was taller than him; maybe he's standing on tiptoe. My borrowed towelling dressing gown swings open and he impatiently folds it over me.

'That's it, don't you see? That's it.'

I can't find the belt of the dressing gown and while I fumble in its folds, he picks it up, knots it tightly, rests his hands on my shoulders.

'Thanks. That's what?'

'If you – or you and I – can't . . . with everything that's

happened, everything we've been through . . .'

'Can't what? I don't have your—' Just in time, I stop the words *desperate need for* and replace them with, '—easy access to emotions. From choice. That's how I work.'

He trumpets his anguish to the low-beamed ceiling. 'That's it!'

Don't get me wrong – I admire Gwyn. He never does things by halves. He's totally present, totally in the moment – but his intensity is exhausting. I find my attention wandering; I wonder if thoughts of mutual between-sheets consolation had been on his agenda . . . and whether it might be worth dropping my guard, just for one night . . . He's passionate, and that is refreshingly novel to me – but as his voice came and went, it seemed another offer was being made, something about knowledge we shared, and an offer to pool our otherness . . . but now I was most definitely asleep, and he gave it up, gently shaking me awake.

We glide along the corridor in the surreal light of the hurricane lantern. I open the door of my bachelor bedchamber, and we suddenly hear it. Someone is crying.

'Maybe we shouldn't intrude—'

He darts me a contemptuous blink. 'That's a child in pain—' He opens the door to Amber and Clover's room.

In the dark, Amber is doubled up in the bed, weeping, still wearing her daytime clothes, a pile of teen magazines slithering from the duvet to the carpeted floor. Gwyn hangs the lantern from a hook.

'Show me.'

She opens her mouth and we both see it. The vicious, too-shiny purple gum, the blue-black cratered molar . . .

'Christ,' says Gwyn, and I don't disagree. 'It's going to have to come out, Amber.'

'Aowh!' howls Amber, and Clover half-awakens, and down the corridor a door opens.

'Amber?' It's Lally, in a toddler-style fleecy pyjama suit, baby-pink, wrinkled and soppy; she takes Amber in her arms.

'I'm going to take it out, Lally. It's infected – the whole gum, everything – look at that swelling—'

'Baby, baby . . .' croons Lally.

Soon the room is full of whispering adult figures, shipwrecked, scared, lost children at a party.

'We can't leave it . . .'

'. . . what about Rescue Remedy . . .'

'. . . with string . . .'

'I'm sure there's a homeopathic thing . . .'

Amber cries, open-mouthed, with pain, and Clover erupts, pointing accusingly at Lally: 'You're her mother! Do something!'

The sibilant susurrations grow and mingle and ebb like the sigh of wave on shingle.

Gwyn, who has left the room, returns with a pair of wicked, uncompromising pliers.

'Oh my god . . .' says Jerry; but Lally has fainted and the rescue remedy is applied to her first, four drops on her tongue, religiously, ritualistically. Then Gwyn stands over Amber, steady, low-voiced.

'. . . hold her mouth open . . .'

'oh God suppose she bleeds . . . ?'

'. . .wider than that, come on . . .'

'NO NO NO . . .' screams Amber, wide eyes disbelieving the size, the gleam, the surgical questing snout of the metal pincers—

'Hold her down—'

'Christ, Gwyn, man—'

'Hold her—'

'. . . fucking don't, man . . .'

'Aaaaa!'

'It's coming – open wider—'

'Aaaa—'

'Good girl, Amber—'

'AAAAA!'

'Got it.'

Amber kicks Gwyn as hard as she can, while Clover

staunches the crimson flow from her mouth with a clean sanitary towel, the first thing she could find. The tooth, a burnt-out firework, trails its bloody comet between the pincer claws. Gwyn is immovable, pragmatic: 'Lally, boil up some salt water to disinfect it. Amber, don't swallow any – spit it all out. Someone see to Ross, I can hear him crying.'

'If you're so fucking clever,' mumbles Amber, bitterly biting on the towel, 'why did you let the others die?'

Rodney is having trouble, sleep trouble. The waning moon elbows him awake. Sweat oils the folds and creases of his neck, his armpits, stains the sheets with the odour of his musk, of his slaked lust. In spite of the unnatural, terrible heat, he is shivering. Outside in the moon-stroked shadows, he is sure nemesis keeps his vigil, coldly omniscient, immortal, crazed with the violence of grief.

Rodney believes in telepathy, dark magics, and death penalties, so it's no idle musing that someone somewhere has drawn a nightmare, a feast of horrors and given the monster his face.

He tosses the sheets aside and wonders whether to look out of the window. In the moonlight he would see clearly the face of the adversary, his destroying angel. Uncontrollably he shivers, writhing, a greying grub consumed slowly, ardently, inside to outside, by his ichneumon parasite.

⁓

They all go back to bed, to sleep; Lally takes Amber, heavily sedated with valerian, to sleep in her bed.

'Gwyn—'

He regards me with a quizzical, a Welsh wizard's, eyebrow.

'Come in with me.' He lets out a breath, deflating like a jester's bladder.

'I don't – I haven't – look, I'm knackered.'

'Me too. No pressure.'

'All right, then.'

Puzzled, he comes into my room. This is something else – not business, not lust – somewhere between the two. I know Gwyn knows. He sees ahead to what's coming. Tonight I want to be with someone who knows.

Without touching, we get in the bed and the candle gutters on the bedside table. The bed is damp, the duvet not thick enough.

'You should be Refs, you lot.'

'Maybe we are. Maybe you are.'

'It wasn't done like that in Ireland. Things were way more improvised – well, chaotic, really.'

'Who said they weren't chaotic here? They sent us letters, of course, to begin with, and we kept ignoring them, and then everything stopped.'

The candle wavers, goes out, with timely symbolism.

'What's going to happen, Gwyn?'

He makes a curious, dragon-like noise in the dark. 'You know as well as I do. Don't you?'

'Can it be worse than this, then?'

He suddenly sits up in the bed, and I am reminded momentarily of Guy and his night terrors in the old days.

'You aren't part of the nightmare, Billie; you're something else – something strange, but you're not part of it.'

I'm very near to telling him what I think I know, but it isn't the time, it isn't right. I've come back for Guy. That was the deal, and though I don't understand how I know that was the deal, it's what I bought.

But Gywn, unquestionably the alpha male in this troop, deserves a gesture, a token of respect.

'Gwyn . . .' Next to me, I hear him suddenly exhale. '. . . how do you lay a ghost?'

My words hang in the air for a radioactive moment. Then I feel his hand gently touch my arm, waiting for me to take it, and I squeeze the broad fingers, unnaturally warm.

'Lay a ghost?' He sounds as if he's smiling, there in the dark. 'Is that how you see yourself?'

'I'm sure of nothing. I can't remember how I got back here. I think everything ended for me. But—'

He puts his head down to my chest. 'You have a heart. You may not want us to hear it beating, but we do.'

I feel defeated. I must be alive. I feel. I feel – hang on a minute – I feel something, and it isn't spiritual. It's something I recognise very well indeed. Gwyn's head on my chest, his abundant dark hair, his strength – suddenly I want to be part of it.

I don't speak again, but move towards his mouth, and, touching breathlessly, strangely, we exchange an aliens' kiss.

We cling to each other in curious marine detachment; molluscs, limpets, rock-bound.

This is not easy, not for me, sharing anything with another hasn't been easy for a while now . . . and I hate the tuning-up, the overture, the dissonant attempt to smother, with muted minor chords, the brassy, self-conscious critic within. Tentatively, hesitantly, we touch, and again, pressing harder now, trying to blot out memory, hoping the sleeping animal will blunder awake . . . and wormlike we wriggle beneath the covers, grunting, sniffing, arousing, procreating; blind foot-soldiers in the war of evolution.

Afterwards, I couldn't sleep. Regret was in it, and self-reproach – but there was something else disturbing me. My body. It didn't feel like my old body. How, in what way, I couldn't articulate. And that disturbed me even more.

I didn't want to wake Gwyn, so I lay staring into the heaving darkness, seeing shadowy faceless figures, nebulous outlines, billowing in all the corners of the room.

'Billie?'

'I'm here.'

'That was . . . strange. Wasn't it?'

'Yes.' He wrapped his hands around my head, pressing his forehead against mine.

'It's better not to think about it. Maybe it's enough that we—'

'No!' He gripped my shoulders in the dark, and I felt his wonderful heat, his passion; but it didn't connect any more, somehow. 'No. That's not what it's for. It has to mean something, not just coupling, like beasts—'

'You're hurting my shoulder.' He let go, instantly contrite, saying, 'I'm sorry. Your feelings are not my business.'

'I'm not feeling anything.'

He sat up in bed again, pulling all the covers off me, and groaned despairingly into the night: 'Then what the fuck are you doing?'

They don't need maps; they sniff and blunder their way through the night, leaving a trail of mashed earth, smashed cars, trashed lives, in their nuclear wake. There is no consensus about what they do, only the vilest will and the most brutish voice and the fastest weapon drive them on, and their dreams are nightmares, and they are getting very close.

~

Alastair brought Guy his breakfast: dry cornflakes. There was no sign of Margaret, but Alastair's hair was neatly brushed, his tie carefully knotted, everything as usual.

'She's a bit under the weather this morning,' he said, attempting cheerfulness. 'Now, let's see that hand. Today's the day, eh? Bandages off after breakfast. After our whisky.'

Time to go. One more day gathering strength, then he would go. Quietly, when they were asleep, so as not to provoke more gentlemanly reproaches, civilised urgings to stay. He knew – had known it all along. They had no food. He was eating their rations, their survival hoard. They were dying so that he might live.

~

Sally is going shopping, even though this thundery and overcast day is giving her a headache. Maybe she'd feel better if she had a gun. Her nerves are stretched with anticipating the ragged, random, ugly termination of her fragile new routine. She's tried to take control of her life, to organise her existence in a way that depends on no one else; she can go for days without seeing anyone. She doesn't miss her friends; she doesn't need a lover. But, unfortunately, she has to eat, and these days, that involves a relationship – in some ways, the most meaningful one Sally's ever had.

It also means getting up early in the morning before the gangs are stirring, and striding, head and shoulders thrown back, convincing yourself you feel good, confident, worth feeding, to the old Tesco's in the High Street, carrying the recycled Asda bags tucked inside her nurse's coat. The Collective knows she's a nurse. They like her strange songs. They know where she lives, and what she'll do for them without complaint or comment, when they come visiting. So it has been decided that she gets food.

There is only one route to the door now; across the old car park, where hundreds of abandoned Volvos, Citroens, Renaults, sensible family estate cars with airbags and steel frames and almost every safety feature, were left in perfect parked order, some driverless, some with a parped figure at the wheel or tumbled into the open hatchback along with the full shopping bags. Members of the collective, all young men of proven fitness (mental and physical) with healthy wives or partners but no children, have reclaimed the shopping, dealt hygenically with the bodies, then somehow winched up the cars into a high barricade all around the building. The huge windows and the front sliding doors have been bricked up – they don't need daylight, they have their own generator.

There is a narrow corridor, as deep as a trench on the Western front, and offering as little protection, leading to the back door – the only door, now. As you walk along it, you can be certain that you are being covered by two guns and that your progress is monitored through binoculars. Although Sally's done this trip a few times, this is still the part that makes her insides squirm. It's the same feeling she had when she was ten and a bigger kid gave her a sudden shove as she sat hesitating at the top of the helter-skelter.

At the door, the rule is that she must stop and wait. A muffled voice asks: 'Name?' and then, having given it, she waits some more.

The door opens outwards and inside Sally catches a brief glimpse of three young men wearing balaclavas and aiming an assortment of guns at her, then another, also armed, steps out. They've got this well sorted now, after a few mistakes in the beginning, a few messy deaths and a few abortive attempts by outsiders to take what they weren't entitled to. They train a lot, they do martial arts and target practice, and their grateful, obedient wives spray themselves with perfumes, mousse their hair, prepare the meals and mop the wide aisles, keeping them spotlessly clean, the trolleys marshalled in tidy lines by the entrance, the dwindling supplies stacked neatly on the shelves in their correct places, just like the old days.

'Please can I have something?' This is the only question you're allowed to ask. Shopping lists are not permitted. Specific requests are against company policy. Any refusal of what's offered means you won't be allowed back.

Today, something's wrong. Usually there's a nod here, or a bag of stuff appears and you grab it and run. The young man at the door lowers his gun. He makes an embarrassed little move, as if he would go back. He clears his throat.

~

'The babies want to know if you'll help them,' said Jerry at coffee time, 'they want to do a puppet show.'

Holly dumped a cardboard box at my feet. It was full of toys: dolls, teddies, furry animals and dead, mass-produced, characterless, limp puppets.

'Have you got a story?' I asked. Without consulting Carly or Kyra, Holly nodded importantly.

'It's called *The Bad Sheep*. And I'm the bad sheep.' She held up a sheepish puppet. 'I eat the snake. And Kyra's the snake—'

'No, not the snake,' interrupted Kyra.

'You have to be because Carly won't talk—'

'Carly can be a quiet snake, can't she?' Jerry tried to intervene, and Holly shot her a dismissive glance.

'No, Carly's got to be the Baby.'

'What do you want me to do?' I ask, easygoing, aunt-like.

'You know about puppets?'

'A bit.'

'You show us what to do, then.'

I spend the morning helping them make a puppet booth out of furniture, cardboard and curtains. Then we rehearse. Then we perform *The Bad Sheep*, for an audience of over-enthusiastic, uncritical, mostly stoned, adults.

This, this isn't threatening; it's as far removed from my old life as Galway is from Southwold. It's been over a year since I waggled a dolly. This shouldn't hurt, not at all.

But as I slip my fingers into the flap of flabby material and up into the too-heavy, disproportionate head, and the thing twitches and postures, mouth quacking, eyes darting from child to adult, I have to force the screen in my head to white-out, lead the mental projectionist away from the madly spinning reel, and bite down my urge to re-enact a moment of personal history that has no place in a children's puppet show.

'Billie, that's incredible!' All the grown-ups are transfixed, as they always are when the little dolls begin their waggling, seduced and infantilised by their absurd vitality. 'You really make it seem like they're alive. Look, Carly, look at the crocodile – isn't he scary?'

'It's not a he,' I say, snapping at Jerry with the shiny leprous green snout, 'it's a she.' Then Carly amazes and delights us all with a loud shout of 'Bad Thing!' – the first words she has spoken since her parents died – and we all agree that puppets are a wonderful means of communication.

Later on, after the show is finished and the tiny artistes have been applauded and rewarded, alone in my room, I tilt my head back, close my eyes and allow her to mushroom into existence, to take up her old semi-detached residence in my visual cortex. I kept no photos of Lola. I didn't need to – she was me, an incarnation of me that Guy helped to birth, maybe to love. Only Guy and his equivalent man-made incarnation could understand us.

Lola and Desmond were two massive Ids, blissfully unconstrained by social boundaries; they squeaked out their truths, shallow and infantile as they often were, they ventilated every thimble-sized emotion, whacking each other with passionate abandon and rolled-up newspapers, they sang and danced and lived in a miniature happy-ever-after, and in that daily vicarious transaction Guy and I fooled ourselves we were connecting. In the drama of life, puppets and their wagglers give us the text. It's our job as grownups to decipher the subtext. Or not, as we choose.

For five long years I was that creature twice daily on Southwold beach, and she was my evil twin, my inner child. Guy and me. Desmond and Lola. They never looked like much – a sponge and a dolly. Sexless and of no determinate age, and without our hands inside their spineless cloth bodies, our voices taking on their caricatured squawks and falsettos, they are dead now. Dead as dodos.

SIX

CLOVER IS IN HER BEDROOM upstairs; we suddenly hear her scream: 'Gwyn!'

He's not here; he's outside, working somewhere. I foresee another unsightly medical emergency – childbirth, amputation, removal of appendix – and wonder if this time I can have more of a backstage role, filling kettles and fetching hot towels.

Clover explodes down the stairs, screaming: 'They're in! I can see them, in the wood. Hundreds and hundreds of people – oh, Rose, it's awful, find Gwyn!'

Rose grabs the walkie-talkie, but can't get through.

All of us adults shrink as we look at each other, leaderless.

I hear Amber playing the piano in the playroom: 'Pop goes the Weasel.' The little ones are laughing and skipping about.

Jamie goes upstairs with binoculars while we women lean on the Rayburn, heat-seeking, comfort-seeking.

'How long have we got?' says Lally.

I say, unwittingly parroting the government Eppie booklet: 'Well, we definitely shouldn't panic. That's the worst thing we can do.'

Rose dismisses me, her beautiful eyes dead with contempt. 'Gwyn knew this was coming. That's why he checked the wall every day. That's why we had George.'

'Where the fuck is George?' says Jamie, coming down the stairs faster than I've ever seen him move and pulling on his nicely-worn old brown leather jacket.

They all pick up tempo and begin scurrying from room to room, grabbing photos, trinkets, babies, talismanic protections. The women and children go upstairs to the furthest room. Jamie makes a barricade at the foot of the stair and throws some brooms and a pickaxe onto the landing. He bolts the outside doors.

We are officially at war.

Under pretext of searching for Gwyn, I go to the barn and reclaim my bagman's uniform, pulling off the clean, natural fibre jeans, pure cotton underwear, and all wool sweater I was lent. I don't know exactly what I must do, but first I need to melt, disappear into the morass, be merely part of the general septic flotsam in this river of nastiness.

As soon as I'm re-dressed, I hurry out into the woods. Already things look different. Plants are flattened and blackened as if burnt, stray branches are ripped, shock-white from their sockets, and soggy paper, bright plastic litter and a scattering of random possessions mark the point of entry of the enemy, the warring tribe.

There is a woman squatting under a holly bush; she is having a crap and smoking a filter cigarette at the same time. She thrusts her face towards me, chin lifted, flaunting her black eye with puny, victim's aggression. Still squatting, she gives me two fingers and I mildly respond in kind. When she gets up and walks away from her business, I see the tangled, thread-like moving masses in the shit.

I follow her and others to a clearing where there is a higgledy-piggledy assortment of tents and rough benders. Kids are screaming, dogs are barking, engines are uselessly revving. One man lifts his arm to belt his woman, his slit, fully across the face. She staggers back, bleeding at the corner of one eye, uncomplaining, and the next moment has upended a bottle of a foul-smelling liquid over his head.

A comparative silence falls as a hard man, their king, appears on his enormous black steed, and it paws and curvets on the peaty ground, nostrils flaring. Small children fall back, terrified of the hooves and the teeth and the rolling eyes. I hear his name, spoken in whispers. Mart. Mart is here. Mart will sort everything.

Then I see Gwyn, alone, also riding a horse; the unimpressive grey pony with the white flash he usually takes around the perimeter each morning. He approaches while the new King waits, with disdainful, absurd courtesy, his face an omniscient, smirking mask.

Gwyn halts the pony. He and Mart begin talking, and suddenly the crowd is jostling and heaving to get closer, to hear the parley. With a heavy, squishing wallop, a soiled baby's disposable nappy, badly aimed at Gwyn's head, falls against his leg and slithers slowly earthwards. There is triumphant, jeering, venomous laughter from a hundred fag-fogged throats.

Mart acts as if the crowd does not exist. If they existed he would have to pretend he controlled them, and he is too intelligent to suffer that humiliation.

Suddenly it is finished. Gwyn makes a furious gesture of his hand. Mart shrugs. Gwyn turns in the saddle. His voice is huge in the dim light of the clearing. His hair is wet. His face is granite.

'I tell you what I told him,' he says, and they all hear, not in silence, unwillingly. 'I know we've got things you want. You can take them if you like. In this place, we don't use weapons to kill people. But if you take this by force, if you lay waste the land and kill us all, you'll be the losers. We know things, see. We know . . . how to milk cows, how to make bread – when did you last eat fresh bread?'

There is a muttered obscene joke in the crowd and they roar their approval of the interruption.

'We know how to keep seed for vegetables, look after the goats and the cows, make sure there's enough for next year. It's all right here. We can survive – all of us. But if you can't see beyond the next day, the next week, well, it's your funeral.'

They let him go because, although they heard, they haven't understood a word, except that he is beaten, he is talking surrender, and soon the big house and the squirty imitation cream on the tinned fruit salad of life will be theirs.

Gwyn's lips move; I guess he is speaking in Welsh, but not for them, for himself. To them, he is already dead, and what can the dead teach us? He turns the pony; it walks away. Gwyn doesn't look back.

Excitedly, the rabble presses around Mart, jabbering, pulling at his clothes. His lieutenants use their whips. Their liege lord retires to his pavilion, and his squires, his lackeys, follow, spitting threats at the serfs and villeins who would be privy to their private deliberations.

I slink around the perimeter wall, smashed now in many

places. At the lodge gate George still stands sentinel, but when I get closer I see that he is tied to the gatepost, the features of his face no longer there, hacked off, inartistically re-arranged, a trail of bullet holes across his chest and around his trouser crotch a dark, bloody stain.

Inside the lodge cottage that used to be his, there is a couple engaged in violent, loveless, high-decibel screwing; I can hear them at it and so can the four or five filthy little children in the mud outside who are tormenting an exhausted kitten. I think about saving it, truly I do, but in the end I turn and walk away.

~

Guy fits the puppet on his hand, and Alastair's face lights up, like a little boy who hasn't had any treats for far too long.

'How does it feel?'

Guy wants to say, *it feels poisonous, inevitable, like what I deserve, like dead yesterdays.* What he actually says, politely: 'It feels fine.'

'Hallo, Alastair,' says Desmond's voice, 'my, you're a big boy, aren't you? When's your birthday . . . ?' The little mouth flaps open and shut, open and shut; the cheeky freckled face mugs and smirks with latex enthusiasm; the unfocused, too-bright-blue eyes stare in no direction, in every direction, their lashless rubber lids moulded forever open, pointlessly vigilant.

'I say, Desmond,'—and Alastair no longer looks at Guy, his patient, his creation; like all the others he has eyes only for the appealing, lopsided schoolboy face, the tousled mop, the miniature school cap sewn through the skin of the latex skull, the celebrity in short trousers—'do you think you could come and cheer Margaret up?'

'Cheer Margaret up,' says the falsetto, rallying little voice with a hint of salacious rib-nudging, 'cheer her up, I should say, we can do that, can't we? Desmond and big Dez, a wow with the ladies. I'll tell her a fairy story and he can give her one, oops what am I saying, give her a lullaby, that's what we meant, isn't it Dez? Just let me get my hands on her, she'll never be the same again . . . you keep your eyes open, you could learn a thing or two . . .'

He won't shut up now, not ever. Alastair is smiling; his face looks less strained and he's leading them into Margaret's bedroom, and Guy is back on the vicious old helter-skelter, fast and furious, and the voice in his head throbs like the pain in his useless left hand.

Margaret is lying down, and Guy sees she has been crying, though she makes an effort to smile and raise herself up when the boy Desmond arrives with his merry banter and his creator, Big Dez, his perpetually puzzled sidekick.

She tries not to use her hankie, not to sneeze or cough, because everyone knows what the signs mean, these days.

It's taken a while, but the thing has finally got her where it wants her. Not easy, knowing that you'll be dead in a few days – painfully, emptily, parped. Maybe Alastair has saved some drugs. Maybe they'll go together.

'Now, Margaret,' Desmond is whispering, nuzzling at her breasts under her nightgown with his ingenuous little boy's wide-open mouth, 'I've got a suggestion for you . . .' And she tries to laugh, she smiles, and Alastair grips her hand as if she is drowning, which of course she will be soon.

'I can't thank you enough,' Alastair says later, back in Guy's room when the boy Desmond has been put to bed in a suitcase. 'Seeing him again, hearing his voice – it brings back good memories for us. I never thought we'd be entertaining a celebrity in our own home. How's the hand? Was it painful for you, doing that?'

Guy lies, convincingly, as he always does: 'No, really – didn't hurt at all.'

~

Rodney is fluttering with fear. He knows now the searing certainty of personal, private violation. Someone has been in his flat, has searched it, and has left a message on his escritoire. Folded, vellum notepaper. With a lurching heart he knows it is the little girl's father. He is going to torture his daughter's torturer slowly to death; the death of uncertainty, the death of the hypnotised rabbit caught in the glare of the headlights. He won't actually have to do anything. Rodney will do it all himself. Look at him now, circling round the letter, his day's business quite forgotten – even his cuff-links aren't fastened properly. With a trembling hand he reaches towards the paper but can't quite, doesn't quite have the guts to pick it up . . . yet read it he must. Pandora's curiosity has him in its fatal grip, and another volition seems to take over, and Rodney feels his bowels loosening as he opens the creamy-smooth paper.

'*You have come to our notice*,' is all it says. Feverishly he reads and re-reads, trying to find more, but there is no more, except the inescapable horror that someone knows, maybe has watched him taking his necessary pleasure, watched and judged. And how many times? How many operations, how many little binbagged bodies have been logged and counted, and how many damning, coal-black, soul-black marks have been heavily scored against his name?

He moves to the nearest chest of drawers and tugs it open. The banknotes, complacent virgins, lie between their immaculate sheets. This should reassure, but it doesn't. They did not come for his treasure. They, the unknowns, have a specific, incomprehensible, customised goal.

Rodney is more than scared now; he is spasmed, incoherent with panic. He is not safe in the flat; they can get in. Not safe in the street, nor in the park. They see him, everywhere he goes, they see him and now they intimately know him.

'You have come to our notice.'

So there is more than one of them. He is outnumbered, outclassed; in the spectrum of refined torture he is merely a beginner, a clumsy novice. He gazes out of his window, and under the gravid, dispassionate skies he sees a thousand red-eyed vengeful beasts sharpening their claws.

⁓

Sally does not usually smoke, but today is different. It's been a difficult day for her. Grubbing around in the bottom of the old orange box she keeps vegetables in, she finds some papery, faded onion skins resting on a layer of dirty newspaper. She tears off a small strip of the paper, not bothering to look for a cleaner piece underneath, and begins to shred the skins, stopping every now and then to bite her nails, already bitten to the quick.

Lucky for her, she still has matches. The home-made cigarette flares, then goes out. Patiently she relights it. The need to keep it alight suddenly becomes a desperate, physical craving for a comfort she doesn't usually permit herself.

No food. There is no appeal. It's been decided. And they

don't give reasons. The guns have their own totalitarian logic. And Sally can't help thinking back to what she's done for them, what their clean, obedient wives won't do – and she can't help feeling cheap. She's trying to remember if there was ever a time when she could have made a different choice, if there was ever a time when she despised and loathed herself a little less than she does at this moment.

This unattractive reverie is broken by a polite tapping on her front door. It's not the hearty thumping of the usual customers, it's a shy, hesitant knock that almost asks to be ignored – and for that reason she does not ignore it.

Standing on the doorstep in the chill early evening, shivering a little, is the young man from the Collective. It's the same one who sent her packing this afternoon. When Sally sees what he has inside his jacket, she lets him in and slams the door.

'I can't stay long.' He unpacks the plastic bag, and her stomach tightens, almost nauseated at the unexpected sight of food. 'I – look – the thing is, I—'

Sally draws on her pathetic cigarette, in her mind's eye a vision of the bottle in the cupboard, its liquid hospital oblivion depleted now to a final few inches. Sally does not scream or cry, she simply says, 'Don't talk. Do you want to go upstairs?' It hurts more than a slap in the face when he recoils, putting up his hand as if to ward her off.

'God, no! That isn't why I came—'

Sally chokes on his pity, the words stick in her throat, the self-esteem that should guide her hand to fling the groceries past his retreating figure as she slams the front door on him is muted – maybe was never there. But something must happen; this is definitely a watershed for her, for him.

'I'd better get back—' Then they both freeze, having heard the sounds of fresh arrivals at the front door. No comradely knocking this time, but army boots skilfully applied until the door bursts open and they jostle their way into the kitchen. They grip the youth by one arm twisted behind his back, and speak to Sally with humorous contempt, their big mouths smiling. 'Who's a naughty boy then? Felt sorry for the poor old cunt, did we?' As they smile, they put a gun to his temple, and another to his privates. 'You choose, darling. Up or down, up or down?'

Sally avoids looking at his face, his eyes . . . she's been in bed with this, with these . . .

'Take the food. Don't shoot him. Please. I'll – I'll sing for you.' They laugh – oh, how they laugh. Yet they did love her songs, once upon a time.

'Shoot me. It's my fault, not his. Shoot me.' This time they don't laugh, but tut-tutting, give her to understand that this is not an option.

'Waste of bullets, we don't shoot fucked-out cunts, you know that. Now – up or down?'

⁓

There's a massive pot of hot coffee on the Rayburn, and we are glugging it virtuously, thirstily, like recently recovered alcoholics. I'm pleased with the hippies; on the whole, they are remaining true to their 'live and let live' philosophy, even under siege by the powers of darkness as they appear to be today. And, though they are a group with colourful imaginations, they haven't gone in for melodrama, not as yet. We are silent for at least ten minutes. Then Jerry's voice, a croak, metallic, prescient: 'They won't let this house stand, they'll tear it down brick by brick.'

'They're only people!' shouts Rose, looking to me for support. 'They're only people and they've been through hell.'

'They are the inheritors . . .' intones Jamie, who greatly misses *Dr. Who*, which was actually brilliant, especially with a tab of acid or a line of coke, or, in harder times, a spliff juiced up with morning glory seeds.

'He said we have to hand over the slits. Not the old ones, the fuckouts. Those.' Gwyn nods briefly towards Clover and Amber. 'The babyslits too.' He indicates Holly.

'F-for what?' falters Lally, fingering her crystal.

'You know for what. They'll have to kill Jamie and me first. If we try and get away we'll all be shot, for sport,'—to Jamie—'they've got guns, and cars, most of them.'

'But why? Can't they see what they're doing?' Lally tugs so hard at her crystal that the thread snaps. A smashed rainbow lies on the stone floor. Someone gasps. It's a bad omen.

The hate was always there, the anger, the blinkered, annihilating greed. Sheathed and cloaked by a hundred rage-baffling diversions; opiates, addictions, reality TV, tabloid fantasies, blogs, smartphones, social networking sites . . . All gone now.

Jerry nods. 'They've always been out there, and we've been lucky, that's all. The ones who died . . . they're better off than we are now.'

A silence falls, of unshared thoughts; then suddenly there is a cold black well of bitter water into which we all stare. Silence is broken by Kyra, who is sitting on the floor playing with a puppet, a furry spider; she laughs.

'There's some stuff in the garden—' begins Rose, then she draws the adults nearer and they whisper, and Clover clings to Amber, too drunk on the drama to be scared.

Kyra climbs on my lap, and sits bolt upright, unblinking, her no-colour pale hair falling in her eyes. Her stiffness, her lack of flexibility, suddenly seeming to me like strength.

The whispering group breaks, and outside we can hear a drunken argument, ended by a single gunshot.

'Okay, everyone,' begins Rose, as calm as a washday Monday morning, 'Clover, Amber, are you listening? This is our choice. To play their stupid game, to stay until they break in, break us . . . let them do what they like with us . . . with the house . . . and the babies . . . or we can—' Her confidence drips away and she looks for help to Gwyn. Gwyn is kind. He knows. He's always known.

'Look, it's like this, see? I'd rather go and be with Bethan and the others.'

Clover screams, then tries to gag herself with shaking fingers. This is grown-up business, this; it's partly her fault for being a slit. She and Amber are the ones they have plans for.

'Well, what would you rather?' pursues Gwyn, targeting their shocked and childish faces, and now his voice is ancient, priestlike, heavy with fury. 'At least we have a choice, a tiny choice. The little ones, they'll come with us, they won't know what's happening. Rose knows how to do it, what plants to pick. It won't taste very bad, and it will be quick.'

'Oh my God,' says Jerry softly, 'this is for real, isn't it?'

Guy and Alastair have finished the last bottle of whisky, sitting in the kitchen. It's the first time Guy has been downstairs since he arrived, and it jolts him backwards into a world of quiet, professional mediocrity, like the grey good taste of a solicitor's purring Mercedes, the mindless sameness of a chartered accountant's lunchtime sandwiches. The kitchen is unimprovable, forgettable, spotless. No food has been cooked in here for quite a while.

'I understand you going,' Alastair is saying, generous and fair-minded to the last, 'after all, you could catch—'

'No. It's not that.' Guy feels his hand twitching inside the puppet, the mouth jerking with impatience. 'You know the thing that's wrong with me, Alastair. I can't catch the fucking plague, I don't understand why not, but I can't. I've no immune system left, nothing makes sense, all I want is to go.'

To his horror he sees tears in Alastair's grey-blue eyes and quickly his hand shoots up, involuntarily vertical, and the idiot sybil comes to life and launches into another monologue: 'Got to run, old boy, but I need a motor; got any transport? Thinking about it you must have, after all, how did we get here, it wasn't a piggy-back, that's for sure. And now all the whisky's gone there isn't much to stay for – we always leave the audience wanting more, don't we Dez – pardon him, he's a bit of a party pooper – well, we can't choose our parents can we? Not that I'm saying we're related, only in a manner of speaking—'

Guy pulls the puppet off his hand, squeezing its neck with his remodelled fingers. He had thought it would be less unbearable with the arms and hands immobile, hanging by Desmond's side just as his own left hand hangs now, fingers permanently crooked like a dead starfish, but it wasn't. The ghastly vivacity of the head, the rubber face, reminds him now of a drunk at a party who stands next to you telling jokes while you puke all over his shoes.

'Maybe there's a bicycle I could—'

'Don't be silly,' says Alastair, gripping the arms of the chair, tempted by unmanly, seedy thoughts about what he will do when Guy has gone and Margaret is dead, 'you're in no fit state to undergo that kind of exertion. Where do you want to go?'

'Back. Where you found me.'

He nods, defeated. 'I'll take you in the trap. We can do it easily. It's only ten miles from here. I'll get the map and show you.'

Now I'm on the road again, but not alone this time. The two of us left hurriedly in the darkness, waiting until the blood-slaked beast snored beside the ruins of the fire; the smouldering trunk of the four-hundred-year old oak that this morning had stood regally secure, metaphysically wise. Tomorrow more trees will die, and more the next day, and life will go on, until it stops, and who cares, anyway?

We've seen some horrors, now, my companion and me, things we'd rather not speak of, but which it would be cowardly to conceal. If we're chronicling the end of human history, it would hardly be fair to skip over the unfunny bits.

They broke into the house just before darkness, having sent in a few warning missiles: rocks crashing through the windows, burning bits of non-biodegradable stuff that somebody inside the house quickly put out while Rose stirred the cauldron. She took her time; the doors and windows were locked and barricaded; on the last day of his life, her Jamie had worked as fast and tirelessly as Gwyn. They had all worked; the women's hands were blistered and rough too. It was a triumph, if a bitter one.

She added blackcurrant syrup, honey and orange flower water. She sieved, she stirred again, scented the vapour, but did not drink.

They knew without asking that I would not go on this journey with them. And I ached for their lost innocence. If I could only have told them something that day. Something real and eternal, a promise of heaven, a place I'd briefly been. But even as I flailed around for words, the images wobbled and flowed from my grasp, like reflections on a river. I was sure there had been lights, moving in sequence, intelligent, purposeful; it wasn't my fever or delirium. And sounds. Not words, but voices, airs, harmonies. But if there was language, it spoke to a deeper wisdom that tenanted my brain, not in my power to understand.

So, more prosaically, I did the housework. I helped Rose. I held the pan while she ladled the stuff into mugs. Carly protested because she wasn't given her own mug with the rabbit on. (Her speech was almost back to normal again). We tried to convince her that today, it didn't matter. But it did matter, of course it did. I was the one who found her rabbit mug.

The clear, crimson liquid smelt like autumn fruits, with the heavy, musky tang of wild honey.

I was standing next to Gwyn as he waited for his turn. My hand could not stop itself from reaching towards, from gently stroking his son's innocent velvety head.

I whispered, as if I was in church, that I would take Ross away from this. I could rescue, and maybe even in time, learn to love him. I wanted to stop the ruby bottle being put to his tiny, perfect, red mouth. But Gwyn shook his head and held him too tight for anyone to get near him.

Clover and Amber were nowhere to be seen, and wouldn't come when we called them. Rose was all for waiting till they came. But Lally, Amber's mother, said softly in her little girl's breathy voice: 'They don't want to play. We have to respect that. I was never a good mother before, maybe I can be now. We have to let them go.'

Gwyn briefly disappeared and came back with blanched face and brimming eyes. He'd put Ross to bed, he said shakily, somewhere no one could ever find him. He did not come to me; he went to Jamie, who, gently as a mother, held his friend till everyone else was ready.

Gwyn said, 'We're going to shut the door now, Billie. We have things to say to each other . . . don't be offended.'

They kissed me, each of them in turn; I fleetingly wished my frozen senses could melt into their warmth. I watched until they lay down together, as we had lain the other evening, comfortably on the old sofa, giving each other cushions, holding each other. From where I stood it looked as good a way as any. Did I want to share their goodbye? Of course not. But what was hurting was that I could not want it – to be like them, stupidly trusting, alive to love. Gwyn especially I regretted. I wanted to melt my awkward, robot self into Gwyn's spirit, to be connected beyond death to that furious, pragmatic Welsh wizard who had always understood, and yet had not run away.

I should have left then, gone with that gentle, easeful picture in my head, but I wanted to see them clear before . . .

By some fluke, only Gwyn was still alive when they broke in. Only Gwyn. It would have to be him, wouldn't it? Hard even for potent, organic poison to damp down the forest fire of his life force. I hid behind some false panelling he had showed me, a secret place that had last been used by a priest or a child playing hide and seek. I couldn't see what was happening, what they were doing to him, but I could hear the sounds of the effort it took, the numbers of men to hold him still while the others grunted about their business.

First they asked him questions, which he would not answer. Then they kicked. I heard the ripping of material; did they strip off his clothes? There was a heavy, rhythmic thudding that went on for a while, and I thought I heard him make a noise: a grunt, a sob. Then the sound of something human cracking against the stone floor, and the sound of a man vomiting up something so terrible his enemies stepped back, appalled. Someone said, 'Poor bastard.'

Then they went away, too scared to finish the work they had started.

I came out of the safety of my hiding place and was glad it was too dark to see properly. He was lying on the stone floor, surrounded by dark pools of stuff, coffee dark, ink dark, and his body was bent backwards, shaped all wrong, and he was still breathing, still alive, if you can call that panting, frothing, torment life. I looked around for something to end the unbearable noise but could find nothing. I knelt down and felt the jagged edges of the hole in his broken skull, imagined I felt it pulsing with warmth; thought of Ross and his exquisite baby head; felt, like a blast of a bomb or a shock wave of an earthquake or the chaos of a cerebral stroke, the mighty pathos of wasted rage, rage too primitive for tears.

'Oh shit, Gwyn . . . oh shit . . . oh shit!'

Funny, isn't it, how I thought I had a way with words. I speak the language Shakespeare spoke, but in the heel of the hunt, as they say in Ireland, sometimes all the meaning is in the gaps, the silences in between.

When it was over, I went back to the secret cupboard and found the small, hunched figure, eyes and mouth tightly sealed, hands pressed against ears, and together, hand in hand, without a sound, we left the house.

It is Kyra who travels with me now; Kyra, aged just ten, who in spite of everything and everyone she was saying goodbye to, chose to come with me. I had dressed her in dark, drab, inconspicuous clothes, and we went out by the open lodge gate; the dead kitten lay in the mud.

'Which way we going?' Now I was going to have to talk, to share, to mother; I wriggle with discomfort like a snake shedding its first skin.

'Don't ask questions. I'll talk when I want to.' Kyra sniffs; in the dark I can't tell if she is crying or not.

'We're safe. Don't worry,' I reassure her fruitlessly, dishonestly; she slips her hand in mine and I take it as forgiveness. I am thinking about the highway, the cars; maybe there is one with some petrol still left in it. I have an idea where to go, the only place left now, but I don't want to tell my companion, to lay it out in the open.

I have a torch now, with a fresh battery, and we study the map. It's a cloudy night with no moon; could rain.

'We'll go for the big road, there might be a car,' I whisper.

But there isn't. We walk, and it rains, and when we are safely distant from the farm we sing about singing in the rain, and we walk, and sing about loving to go a-wandering, and Kyra's voice wanders all over the octave, warbling and various.

'I'm hungry. Hungry to eat now.'

I bite my nails, frustrated. We stop walking, and I get some nuts and withered apples from the pack. Encumbered by a child, my existence can no longer be as hand to mouth, as chancy, as fag-driven, as it was. Daylight finally arrives. We – or I – look at the map. Due to my navigational dyspraxia, we seem to be walking towards Leiston.

I never liked Leiston, even in the old days. It always seemed like the beginning of the London web, the urban ganglands. Now it's dead meat, a satellite in free fall from its parent planet. The shop windows are, without exception, broken, as if a giant has been playing baseball: half-heartedly looted televisions dropped and smashed, microwaves tumbled down carpeted, shat-on stairs. Kyra is fascinated by the electrical goods shops; maybe, coming from her low-tech background, they seem like another planet. I accompany her, uneasily indulgent, as she peers into arctic wastes of white goods – fridges, tumbledryers, washing machines. She's never, as far as I can tell, seen a hairdryer.

Then I hear the familiar, bowel-tickling crunch of boots on broken glass. I grab Kyra, who is usually slow in the reflex department, and we creep into a giant, upright fridge (a very bad idea). The gang kicks, stomps and swears around aimlessly for a bit, then one of them suggests a game; they begin toppling the fridges like giant dominoes. I see a grimy set of fingers curving round our open door, and blow the whistle on our presence.

Awful, this responsibility thing. Before, when these unwelcome interludes intruded, I experienced a single, manageable fear, or nausea, or lust, depending on the personalities involved, but now it's overlaid with complex dualities: resentful protectiveness, neurotic pessimism, laidback fatalism, noble rage and grovelling, opportunistic fawning. It's all Kyra's fault – well, no, not all her fault, it's the hippies' fault too, handing her over to me before they copped out of life, copped off, copped it.

'They're coming,' I say to the gang, hoping they will focus their unattractive skills on me, not Kyra.

'Who?'

'The mad fuckers who killed her parents. They'll have you.'

'You're lying, ya stinkin' Ref,' says gang member number two – there are only three of them, but they're not as cute as my primary school class; over two weeks have passed since then – or is it three? I'm the last person to ask – and we're all wising up; the weakest have gone to the wall, and that includes the ones who like stories about life on Mars with the Royal Family. I debate whether or not to show them my lack of tattoo, but that ritual's dead now; it requires a memory of how civilisation used to work, and these three clearly have none of that.

'I don't care if you believe it or not. If you've any sense, you'll go to London. You stand a chance there. Loads of food, there is.'

'She's a spazzer.' One of them jerks his thumb towards Kyra, and his mates regard her with sandbagged eyes. At least they don't seem to be drunk or pilled, just tired.

'She's a Ref. And a spaz.'

'Yis, thass right,' the oldest one says, grabbing a fistful of Kyra's hair and pulling her head back. 'You're a spaz, in't that right? What are you?'

I see Kyra's larynx bobbing painfully, and, hoping that they haven't checked me out too efficiently in the fading light, I clout his hand away. It's crazy, terminal behaviour – but what can I do? I'm a mother now, obeying new imperatives.

'She can't talk,' I grunt. 'Leave her be.' I adopt a heavy country accent. 'Who's in charge? We need a place to kip.'

Loud, unamused laughter greets this, and a hand reaches into a pocket to produce a knife. I pull Kyra behind me, and kick out at the knife and its owner with my mud-caked, steel-toe D.M.s, the only item of new clothing I brought with me from the farm. The farm. The commune of kindness they called Paradise. Paradise fucking lost. I open my mouth and bellow, screech and howl for a full minute, like any fanged or taloned beast; the sound is so loud it hurts my ears. They are wary, watching me, to see what form my madness will take next.

'Hurt her, and I'll kill you,' I say, and they are satisfied with what they have unleashed, and two of them step back into the shadows. The third, either less gifted in the intellectual arena or more tenacious, lifts his arm to – what? Punch? Stab? I grab his arm; much to my surprise, I've caught him off guard.

He has a tattoo, but he's not a Ref. It's in green ink, and it's homemade. It says, '*WE ARE MENTHOL*'.

'What? What's this?' On his other arm, in blue, '*FUCK OF*'. My noble rage dissolves in an instant as I bite my lip to stop myself laughing.

'That's us,' he's explaining, 'we're the mental gang.'

'And you copied this—'

'Off a fag packet, yeah.' He's so not a threat. He's probably as sick of bloodshed as I am. I let go his arm and he backs away. He's skinnier than he should be, and he looks very tired, as if he doesn't sleep well.

This is the future, then.

After the long night ends, we walk away. Walking is good, is life-affirming, is necessary.

We walk north-east, out of Leiston, into the dawn. It begins to rain. Kyra may be crying; her face is wet. I may not.

Rodney is bad at hiding. He is in an alley, most disgustingly and grossly dirty. There are even some parps lying around the dustbins. But today, Rodney welcomes those parps. He embraces them, smearing their slime all over his immaculate suit – which he now realises is such a giveaway. He voluntarily rubs his nose in this human dirt. He doesn't know who is on his trail right now, how many, how they have sniffed him out. But he can fill in the gaps, his imagination bloats like a cancerous stomach, heavy with the tumour of rumour.

He saw a man this morning, a dark-skinned, short-haired man in a fawn suit, wearing dark glasses. It was her father. Who else could it be? The man was standing in the window of a looted shop, arms folded, looking at him. It was the power of his motionlessness that terrified Rodney. Anyone who can afford to be that still must have a terrible army at his disposal.

Rodney is too old for prayers, though he remembers hearing them when he was stretched across his Nanny's lap, in rhythm with the rise and fall of her High Church coat hanger, spreadeagled over her quivering porky hams, while he lay gagging on the chlorine-bleach fumes of her apron, moistly underlaid with the musky coyness of her intimate talcum powder, her voice droning the cadences of the General Confession, washing away – or at least diluting – the awful wickedness of his secret sins, while the cleansing, comforting, absolving pain that began as a warmth, and hotly grew, and swelled and burst into unbearable, luscious bloom as Nanny's breath grew faster, fiercer, more purifying, took it all away. Until the next time.

It's all so undignified, this way of ending his career, not unlike prison life – though there, at least, money had still worked. Money had bought him books, a desk, occasional bottles of fine wine, and smuggled messages from other investment bankers or insider traders. Only then, of course, he was the insider. Maximum security for three years, marked as a Ref like all the others, not given the so called 'life-saving' shots, the useless flu vaccine that had an unforeseen, unfortunate side effect: it took away those natural human urges leaving everyone still standing a civilised neuter after the holocaust – mild-mannered sheep with no erectile tissue, no desire. But right now, he's wondering if this wholeness of his is worth the candle.

Self-pity overwhelms him as he tries to run, stumbling, flapping, his nose dripping, his eyes red-rimmed. Who'd bother to invest with this risible investment banker today?

Of course they will use their dogs. They know his smell. The whole of London knows his smell by now. He can hide in the sewers, the lavatories, the burial pits; they'll find him. They always do.

~

Walking along the beach; Southwold. Bending like an old man to look at a pebble, pick up a piece of sculpted, white-boned wood. Slow, leisured paces. Stop and sit down, watch the tide. Admire its sameness. Guy is tired. He's made it, where he wants to be, and now he's wondering why he came here, waiting for whatever ungainly death comes to claim him.

It was harder than he expected, saying goodbye to Alastair. Without him around, without his unforced, kindly, unimaginative heroism, self-pity has a field day, and self-absorption fills in the remaining chasms.

He rolls up his trouser and looks at his ankle. It's there. It wasn't there yesterday, but it's there now. Just below the skin: blisters of the colour that old-fashioned actor laddies call 'lake', as they gouge with the orange sticks and twirl and finely sketch in the joke wrinkles and ageing hollows of the face. And now the lake is drowning him, patch by patch, under the powdery flimsy sheen of the skin. Kaposi's sarcoma. Ugliest word in the language, sarcoma. This, then, was what was held at bay so kindly, so magically, by all the tablets he took for years, took for granted. Till they ran out.

There's a scuffling inside his coat pocket; Desmond wants to come out and play. Desmond doesn't know the word sarcoma, or any other words that sting. Desmond's only a boy, with a boy's wandering mind. Guy lets him out and he gazes in freckly cheerful approval at the sea, the stony beach.

'Here, Desmond,' says Guy in his own voice, 'suck on this.' He tilts the face down, and the smiling blue eyes look at the leg, the mortifying patches; the little mouth grins, unabashed: 'Curtains for you, then, Guy old bean. We've had some false alarms but this looks like the business, eh?'

'Not only for me, you stupid little bastard,' says Guy, mashing Desmond's face against the leprous stain, 'don't you get it yet? Don't you?'

~

We walk into the daybreak, Kyra and me, and our slight depression is eased by a fabulous, liquescent sunrise. She is stodgily uncomplaining, her calfless parallel legs stumping tiredly at my pace, refusing to flex at the ankle as other children's do.

'Where we going?' Maybe she's forgotten she's already asked this question, back in the night, when we first hit the road.

'To the sea.'

She fidgets her shoulders. 'I'm too hot.'

We stop and take off some layers and I marvel again at how mothers and fathers ever manage to achieve anything in the lulls between these tedious mandates; dressing, undressing, washing, feeding, distracting.

'What's that?'

The noise grows; now it is unmistakable. The flacking, leathery chopping, the bronchitic whine, as of a sick pterodactyl; the whirling blades pass directly over us, moving eastwards, and, as the sound grows more distant, I dare to lift my head and watch the helicopter banking, hovering, moving southward, Londonward.

'Oh my God.'

Kyra is thinking. 'Looking for us?' She looks at me for confirmation.

'They can't be. Why would anyone be looking for us?'

Kyra's face is scratched by a bramble; I lick my finger and wipe the blood off, as, I suppose, mothers have done down the centuries.

This is bizarre indeed. The world is supposed to have stopped, hasn't it? After the end, do we get the B-side of life, an eternally looping aftermath? And who decides this? What intelligent life form is left who knows how and when it all begins again?

These thoughts too roughly tickle the pusillanimous areas of my imagination, like a boisterous gang of big brothers; they don't know when to stop. A fag would help, would keep this stuff down nicely, but I don't have one. Or a drink. Or, even at this early morning hour – but I can't do that now, I have responsibilities. Failing my usual solaces, it has to be a kip. The next barn, the next wood, the next big car will do.

Nervously, we approach an old Suffolk barn, its ancient wooden shingles painted black, which gives it a menacing appearance; I have a premonition that all over the country parped figures are arising, throwing off their blackened husks, and returning to the rhythm of their tasks of a month ago.

The barn is quiet and smells in a nostalgic way of cows. In one corner, my torch picks out some cleanish bales of straw. We lie down on these, and I listen for any ratlike scamperings and squeakings with a pitchfork nervously, and therefore inaccurately, poised to strike. Kyra is soon snoring beside me; her compact body exudes warmth and I sniff and nuzzle her cool cheek, in a wordless good night. Eventually my weak-kneed vigilance is eroded by half-dreams, dozings, and finally by deep, unconscious sleep.

Give him his due, Rodney has pulled out all the stops. He didn't know he could run so fast or gasp so exotically, or fall so many times and pick himself up and run again so determinedly. Is this prize, life, worth the humiliation, the slog?

Now he's lying face down in a street somewhere, his eyeballs at gutter level, close enough to observe the minutiae of his new kingdom: rat droppings, oily patches of unspeakable nastiness, wet fat turds, rust and corruption and urban, eternal excrement.

He's played out, that's the ugly truth; he's at their mercy now, merely waiting for the bullet, the boot driven between the outspread legs, the gobs, the razorblades.

In a sense, Rodney is asking for it, asking for the exact mode and method to be spelt out, because, as an old hand like Rodney knows, the worst is not knowing, but being forced to imagine. Not yet sentenced, on remand. Awaiting trial. So if, in this direst moment, Rodney oozes lemony tears from every orifice, further polluting the other gutter filth as it swirls towards the grating, to be sucked down into the darkness – well, we sympathise, don't we? We're only human too, we have our little fantasies, our little greeds and needs. We all of us, admit it, feel a little bit sorry for the old banker, the con, the filthy Ref, the dreaming Tiberius.

Suddenly he is jerked to his feet, his arms pinioned. Handcuffs. Dragged, stumbling, off-balance, to a waiting car. Glossy black body, smoked glass windows, and on the side a crest, a heraldic device. Yet another day of joust and tourney would seem to belong to the Black Knight. The car, engine ticking, moves a few inches, stops. They are picking something up, something from the gutter. He is sandwiched between two bodies, his thin thighs intimately squeezed. Laughter. They stuff the gutter thing into his mouth and hold it closed.

The car drives suavely away.

Seven

WE SEEM TO HAVE LOST a day here, maybe slept through it, with occasional fitful wakings and thrashings. I try and rouse Kyra but she is gone, dreaming, her eyes rolling under their short-lashed lids.

Seeking for solitary yet decent amusement, for distraction, I root around in my pack. I've hardly touched the thing since I was at Paradise Farm. The candles are still there, the seaweed isn't – donated to one of the evening soups. The letters – ah, yes, the letters. Only one left to re-read now.

It's a shop-bought card, but strangely apposite, nevertheless. On the front, a marionette with its strings in the act of being scissored by a large and unknown hand, its clown body and long, spidery limbs jumbled and jangled together, its red and white face brutally cheerful. Inside, a hand-drawn cartoon of Guy hanging from a noose. 'Guilty as charged for failing to appear at the hospital,' is the inscription, which, although it doesn't come anywhere near what he owes me, is – in his personal lexicon – a veritable cornucopia of apology. Signed with two kisses. And a G. Not even his full name, which suggests to me he feels just a tad out of his depth.

Is the marionette supposed to be him? Me? Another? How dare he know I was in hospital? A few of the questions I hope to put to him, if he's still with us.

Kyra stretches and stirs, poking out her tongue. Watching her, my self-pity is temporarily abated.

I push the card into a crevice of the straw bale, wondering why I kept it so long, why it bothered me so much. If things had been different, if the world hadn't ended . . . He's done me wrong, all right, but in the bigger picture, can't I let it go and move on?

Kyra wakes up, not beautifully. I wonder if she realises just how unbeautiful she is to look at. She struggles to lace up her walking boots, her mottled, blue-red legs kicking the air with frustration. I ineptly study the map, isolated in my adulthood, my decision-making importance. It's a fuck of a life, being a parent.

I show her where I think we are, where we're going, but of course she's not listening; she's hungry and thirsty. She's also wet herself during the long night; if she had the rare good fortune to be part of a gang now, she'd get called Spaz, Durr-Brain or Pisser.

Our simple survival needs catered for rather inadequately, we set off. I avoid the road, today; I don't trust it. I feel as if someone has applied cardiac massage to the ventricles of London, and the pulsing arteries are once more pumping their poisonous cargo round the invalid or comatose body.

Kyra hates walking across the fields, and moans a lot. I get bad-tempered. We shout. I feel guilty. She sulks. I apologise. She refuses to accept my apology. It's a piece of piss, this parenthood thing.

Ahead of us, suddenly, I see a familiar landmark. Blythburgh Church, sentinel of Bulcamp marsh and estuary, looking as serene as ever, untouched by plague, famine and fire. My breath catches. Shame on me, when stone moves me as nothing human will.

'Look, see that beautiful building? It's a church. Would you like to see inside?'

Kyra stumps along, pouting. 'May there be angels.'

I can't tell if this is a question or a prayer, but it's a miracle for sure that I can tell her, yes, there will definitely be angels when we get there.

I know we will be lucky. I know the doors will open. I know there will be no horrors inside, only bleached wood, light, and silence.

I send Kyra ahead to try the door. If there is a God, He is surely watching this self-pitying atheist seek spiritual comfort, and if I were Him, there would be no room at the inn for me. But could He turn her away?

The door opens, needing only the gentlest touch of a child's hand. We step in, hushed. The air is like a distillation of purest marble. The cedar chest, unmarked, allows us to lift its lid and inhale the fragrance of luxury. The peace I remember is still there, holding, breathless, as if there had never been any world outside.

Kyra is chewing her sleeve. I know she is mortally hungry. Words will not feed her; but they are all we have.

'Tell me a story, Kyra. Then we'll find something to eat, I promise.'

She carefully winds her way along a chosen pew. Looks up. Twenty four pale angels, wings spread, hold steady the flying spans of the roof along the full length of the church. Even from our low perspective we can see the detail of their eyes and hair. Their pursed, peach-hued mouths have never needed sustenance. Kyra smiles, amazingly. Reaches for words. I like the way she contains herself, never asking to be touched or held. Her voice is high and cheerful.

'I will tell you about the Eppie. There was a hospital and there was Eppie inside and Eppie escaped and Jamie said it came from the – from the'—she inhales noisily, concentrating—'the Gova-ment. They send it to poo on us and it is a whole big poo on everyone!' She lets out a scream of laughter, and it resonates round the church, bouncing its echoes off every wooden surface. 'Yes it is! It is!'

I find myself praying for food, in an offhand way. God or no God, we have to survive a little longer.

Kyra demands a story from me in return. In this wholly holy place, I try and frame my truth. Perhaps an angel, hearing it, will descend and give me answers.

'Mm . . . One day I was lost and I was in a big room with lots of people in. They were crying and shouting.'

'Was it the Eppie the same?

'Maybe. And it got very misty in the room.'

'What is that, misty?'

'Foggy. Smoky. I was on the floor, with a blanket, like all of them. A big barn. And everyone was scared and started screaming they must get out. They . . . went away. But I didn't. I stayed there, and some lights came and I got a – I got a kind of a message.'

'What is that, a message?'

'Like a voice in my head, but not with words.'

'Who said the voice?'

'I'm not sure. Everything was too misty—'

'Smoke—'

'Yeah, smoke. And the message said I was to come back here, they could bring me here. I said yes. Then I was asleep. Lights were shining in my dream. And next time I woke up I was in a field.'

'In our field?'

'No, far away. I went to London first. I had to walk, and part of the way I went on a bus with some people, some survivors.'

Put like that, in language a child can understand, helps me remember it as it was. Sadly, it doesn't for a moment help me understand what actually happened.

Kyra is thinking. 'This is a twangly story,' she says eventually, and I have to agree.

There is a light crashing sound behind us. We turn to see a small cloud of dust. A fallen angel. Just one, its face gazing equably up at us from the white-dusted stone floor. Kyra kneels down and traces the angel's lips, and I, succumbing to an appalling moment of dippiness, can only admire the symbolism; an angel from the roof swooping down, trusting itself to the innocent hands of a child.

'Got a funny face,' says Kyra, 'like a pie.'

'Yeah, bloody woodworm,' I say, restored to myself in an instant, 'the silly thing could have fallen on us.'

Blessings on Blythburgh church, though. I could have stayed there longer. It would have meant giving up various things – the search for Guy, the struggle to claim I still exist, things that seemed vital once. But Kyra is practical and her hunger is adamantly of this world. We leave, closing the door gently behind us.

Around lunchtime (ha!) we collapse at the edge of a field where some crows are pecking and flapping. This probably means there's a body somewhere, but we're too whacked to care. Kyra sticks her fingers idly into the muddy soil and finds a golden carrot, rain-washed. We uncover more, excited treasure seekers, and eat as many as we can, elegantly spitting out the gritty bits. I fill my bag. Good humour is restored as we walk along a peaceful by-road, the compromise option that I should have thought about this morning.

'Are we nearly there?' But I'm ready for her, and I make her laugh by asking her exactly the same question simultaneously. Luckily, she has a good sense of the ridiculous, and for a while we play that endlessly enjoyable childhood game of repeating what the other person has just said. The afternoon seems weirdly normal – we could be out for a normal walk, on our way home to a house we know, with lights and warmth.

'Look, see that big sign? S for Southwold. We're here at last.'

'Then I can swim in the sea, can't I.'

'What, now, in this wind?'

She ignores my futile interruption, as she always does. We're getting to know each other's little ways.

'I will swim to a . . . to a land. And I can find my friend. And you have got a friend too.'

'Yeah, I told you about him, the puppet show man.'

'No, not in my story.'

'Oh, right, sorry – didn't realise you were in the middle of a story.'

'And the doves will come. Yes, they will fly to our hands.'

'I like it, it sounds like the Garden of Eden. Do you know about Eden, Kyra?'

Her nose is running; she wipes the snot on her crusty sleeve; she nods. 'Yes, I did go to their playgroup.'

It's an answer, if I can riddle it out. Maybe she means Eden's farm, maybe that's where the playgroup was.

Mothering is coming to me slowly, very slowly.

Rodney has been in sensory deprivation for a while, learning to live with his effluent, his odours, his biology. Thirst is the worst, he finds; at times he even thinks about sucking the embarrassing moisture from his trousers; but he can't do that, actually, because his hands are tied behind his back and poor Rodney is not as lissom, as limber, as he used to be.

Meanwhile, in the top-heavy dark, his imagination is busy doing unpaid overtime; he can't seem to persuade it to take a holiday, even a tea-break. He thinks about Ben, often; he regrets Ben, who looked a little like himself as a boy, and wishes the relationship had been less hurried, less physical. Occasionally he likes to blame his present predicament on the Bens in his life. Sometimes his mouth opens all by itself and a puppylike whimpering drools out, when his mind gets busy with words like punishment, revenge, torture . . .

Yes, Rodney is beginning to understand the benefits of chastity, he's beginning to wish he'd got his shots like the other citizens, the normals.

In the high white tower, in the round room, which is surprisingly close to Rodney's cell, there is another meeting in progress. They meet regularly now, every day, there is so much business to process and things are moving so fast.

'. . . thought he was sound, thought we at least were out of the woods but alas . . .'

'. . . noticed he was a little chesty – last Tuesday, coughed a bit, assumed collar too tight, that's all, but evidently . . .'

'. . . pity, in a way . . .'

'. . . a brilliant mind, originated the old 'Refusals' scheme, great pity . . . not live to see fruition . . .'

'Order, gentlemen, please, order,' says Sir Geoffrey, who seems to have been elected chairman. 'Let's look at the agenda, shall we?'

We took over the first sumptuous-looking empty house we could find on Pier Road, forcing the back door and marvelling that there were no parps there; it was probably an erstwhile yuppies' holiday home, and fair play to them, they even had redundant electric blankets and long life cartons of delicious orange juice.

We shared a big double bed that night; Kyra said she wanted to, and we'd got into a married couple's routine of after-lights-out news roundups of the day, plus we had both got used to the nocturnal snufflings and shufflings of another warm body, without which it would be hard to get to sleep. Oh, and bedtimes were when I was teaching Kyra to read. She had one book in her pack – a picture version of Peter Pan. She could already recognise P for Peter, H for Hook and M for mermaid, as well as her name written on the flyleaf. Yeah, I know, I was totally naïve in imagining that reading would still, no matter what happened next, one day be of some use to her; but give me a break – it kept me happy.

We were up early – way too early for me, but Kyra was champing at the bit, ready for the beach. And, as soon as I had levered myself from the horizontal and taken on a semblance of humanity without even a cup of tea, so was I.

We went the long way round, Kyra pointing happily at P for Parking signs, and at one that she said was H for Hook. I steered her away from that, towards the beach, the north end, furthest from where Guy and I used to put up our booth.

I didn't expect to find Guy immediately (and maybe I didn't want to), and I certainly wasn't going to walk the entire length of the beach calling his name like a pathetic abandoned orphan, so we went wherever she wanted to go. We started by the pier, which had been thoroughly trashed as it was way too colourful and appealing to leave alone. I followed Kyra down to the beach, and we made castles and moats, digging in the coarse sand with our fingers, finding shells, throwing stones into the sea. Until I noticed her.

A woman in a blue coat, standing just too far away for me to ask her what the fuck she was doing, standing, staring at us. She had the nervous, preoccupied air of someone who, having made a decision, was too spineless to carry it through. As you can see, I disliked her on sight.

Not so Kyra. She turned in the very act of stone throwing and made a merry gesture of encouragement to the stranger, grinning and accidentally letting fly the stone, which whizzed past my right ear.

Cursing her hippy upbringing, which had left her with such hopeless optimism about adults and their motives, I grabbed her hand and we lumbered slowly over the stones. As we approached the gooseberry, she looked relieved, but still, to my eyes, furtive. Kyra said I was holding her hand too hard. I let go and she went straight to Mrs Weird, patting her coat and sniffing her as she usually did with newcomers, to establish contact. To my horror, I saw the woman's fingers tenderly stroking my girl – my girl! and her tangled locks. A passionate pang – could it be jealousy? – smote me amidships.

'You've got lovely hair,' her first words were – not to me, of course. To me she said, 'I'm a hairdresser.'

There wasn't much I could object to there, surely? She was smiling at me now, a shy and desperate smile. She pointed up behind her.

'That's my house. Sea View. Not very original, I know.'

Look, why not assume she was a perfectly nice, ordinary woman who wanted to befriend us? What worm was gnawing in my bosom?

Kyra was pulling her back towards the sea, urging her to

come and throw stones. With every fibre of my being I did not want her to come and throw stones, but seemingly, I was no longer in charge.

'I used to bring my children here,'—she was pretty good at skimming stones, a lot better than me, curse her—'before the . . . before.'

So she was a mother. Maybe that made it better – no, it didn't, it made it worse, because she was a proper one and I was only rehearsing myself into the role.

'How many children?' was the most neutral thing I could ask.

'I had five.' She stopped skimming, and so did Kyra, lifting her ingenuous, trusting face to drink in this total stranger's tale of tragedy, for such it could only be. 'They were quite small, really. The youngest was three. The oldest one was just eleven.'

I wondered, hoping against all logic, if she was obliquely begging. A made-up tale of such tragic proportions could only be the prelude to some request.

Kyra was looking at me, and I ungenerously frowned back at her, knowing that this adult stuff demanded an adult response, which made me feel all the more like an upstaged, sulky teenager.

'I am sorry,' I said, as sincerely as I could.

'You're lucky your little girl survived.'

Ah. Now I was in a dilemma the like of which I had never experienced in all my life. The reluctance to come clean! What was that about? I looked conspiratorially towards Kyra. Maybe I should simply breathe and relax, let her tell whatever version of our story came to her.

'My name's Sylvia,' the bereaved hairdresser went on, 'would you like to come up to my house? I've got lots of toys up there.'

By now, Rodney has been through the mill; interrogations, isolation, sleep deprivation, prison-type food and water served in grey plastic containers by sneering warders, and he's beginning to be aware that he may be in the hands, not of a law and order brigade, the morality vigilantes, but some eccentric vivisectionists with a taste for bizarre human experiments. If this was justice, surely by now he'd have been scrubbed with cold water and given the humiliating prison dungarees and striped shirts, which make all cons look like refugees from a children's theatre company, but paler and less smiley. No, if this was a regular arrest, he'd surely have been charged with something by now. Rodney has no inkling that he is part of a wonderful new kaleidoscope, an intricate arrangement of Chinese boxes that will eventually reconstruct a tidy new reality.

Eventually, when the Interim Committee has decided, and voted, and had time to pat themselves on the back, Rodney is frogmarched into the round room. His eyes water, unaccustomed to so much light; he feels the swoop and belly-tug of vertigo; from the vantage point of the white tower he can see all over London. He tries to take in what seems to be happening: businessmen, papers, pens, after-shave, maybe even a hint of cigar smoke in the air.

'Do take a seat.' The tone is affable and courteous enough, but Rodney's knees are trembling under the table.

'Welcome to our little group. I expect you'd like a bath and some clean clothes?'

He doesn't know what the right answer might be, or what the penalty for a wrong one could be, so he makes a strangled, half-affirmative noise.

'Splendid. That will be arranged, as soon as certain matters are dealt with.'

Rodney hears his own voice floating upon the scented air, toneless, disembodied: 'What do you want of me?'

'Everything, my dear fellow. Body, mind and soul. You have been chosen.'

'Chosen? For what?'

'Remember how you used to choose? Your methods were unscientific, but effective. We studied your techniques.'

The faces round the table are heavy and accusing now; gone are the smiles.

'I'll – I'll confess. To anything. Tell me what to say. Tell me what you're going to do with me.'

Silence, and the atmosphere is heavy with the ghosts of little children, whose blanched faces press in on Rodney's inner eye, heavy as sin, wordless, anaemic, unblinking.

Sir Geoffrey whispers to a flunkey who stands just behind him. A mirror is brought and Rodney sees what he has become, and the grey tears well in his sick, sinful old eyes.

'Are you going to execute me?' he says, in his cultured, dispassionate drawl.

'Dear me, no.' Sir Geoffrey, chuckling, invites laughter around the table. 'We're going to make you our new Prime Minister.'

⁓

Okay, so she wasn't making it up. She showed us the bedrooms, the natural-looking, touching (to a less cynical pair of eyes) disarray she hadn't had the heart to tidy since they all so abruptly left her. She showed us the photographs, told us their names and ages; the very walls of the house echoed with their dead voices. Every so often she wiped the tears running steadily down her cheeks with the sleeve of her teeshirt, but absently, as if they were someone else's.

She was not from Southwold originally, but from Birmingham, came here on holiday, fell in love with Eddie, who worked in Morrison's supermarket in Beccles. A good man, it would seem, with more than average foresight, who on his last day at work – and the penultimate of his life – had thought of his family and filled his little van with non-perishable food.

In the twins' (yes, she had seven year old girls) bedroom, Sylvia showed me their chest of drawers stuffed with crisps of all flavours – their favourite food when alive, the subject of fierce family battles, ('Though I wish I'd let them eat all the crisps they wanted now'). In return for all she shared, she seemed to expect nothing back from me. I wondered if her kids had ever seen our beach show. Adults never usually noticed us, they fixated on the puppets.

She had a stash of tinned milk, which interested Kyra greatly. She'd never seen milk in such a form, nor the massive plasma screen telly, nor the dinosaur rows of kitchen appliances. As she worked her way through all the flavours of crisps, Sylvia and I drank tea (she had discovered that if you leave teabags in cold water overnight, the result is a species of tea), which, along with some surpisingly crisp ginger biscuits, helped to lubricate our social situation.

'I think we've turned the corner,' says our would-be friend. 'There are signs of things getting organised.'

—

After Rodney has been introduced to the Interim Committee he is taken away for remodelling. Not the surgical kind, only cosmetic: a bath, shave and hair-cut, his nose-hairs trimmed away, his teeth scraped and polished and his pouched cheeks patted and creamed into that unnatural, glossy sheen that the very rich exude, living the entirely wholesome, indoor lives they do.

A tailor measures him. A secretary brings him a leather-bound diary and a list of appointments. His little particularities are noted. Lapsang souchong is obtained, and a pair of silver-backed hairbrushes. He learns that he will not be returning to his flat, but that the currency will be undisturbed, left in vaults. It won't be needed in the new order, probably not ever, he learns at one of the all-day committee meetings; there is an international plan to squeeze out the ineptly corrupt bankers like his former self, and use other tokens for currency – oil (or its new substitute), or armaments, or something very simple and in short supply, such as units of people. He won't have a say in this, of course; he's not considered important enough to have a vote.

He is to live in the new Prime Minister's House at Kensington. He is to be under scrutiny, every minute of every day and night. His private life is, for the moment, to be chaste.

He asked if he could have the flu jab, the passion killer. He wanted never again to feel the tyranny of lust but they told him it would not be an option at this stage. He guessed this was part of his penance. His tattoo, at least, was skilfully removed by a team of cold-eyed, taciturn consultants.

His dreams, his fantasies, will be monitored from now on by a committee of psychologists who may or may not apply appropriate therapy, or even medical treatment. A speech therapist from Yorkshire who reminds him of his Nanny gives him exercises to strengthen his flabby labials, correcting his tendency to drool when agitated.

His past is to be eradicated, or re-written. And Rodney agrees; docile as a bunny, he signs, in triplicate, documents to this effect. He even changes his name. Rodney is undergoing a rebirthing.

EIGHT

THEN SOMETHING TERRIBLE happened. When I woke up, late next morning, Kyra wasn't there.

Her clothes and little pack were gone. Her shoes, everything.

I lumbered out of the house, into the garden, into the street, I began to shout, to call her name, to swing my head wildly, like an orang-utan, from side to side, hoping to catch a glimpse of her stalky, blue-anoracked figure.

I returned to the house and grimly ransacked it for fags and booze. (Didn't find any fags.) I visited Sylvia's house immediately, of course, and she let me search it from top to bottom, in a jealous cold rage. I refused her appalling simulacrum of tea, and her timid, utterly inappropriate suggestion of a haircut, and eventually her quiet insistence that she did not know where Kyra was, and her (angrily rejected) offer to help me look, persuaded me to leave her alone.

I went back to my house and waited for hours, hoping like a desperate child on Christmas Eve that the unbelievable would happen; she might come back. Kyra, the elliptical, the extraordinary, the child of light, had made her choice: she had rejected me.

I wasted a day in bitter reflection, drinking appalling German wine and, finding that Sylvia had been horribly perceptive, took a rusty pair of scissors and cut my hair quickly and brutally, occasionally glancing in the mirror and not caring what I saw.

My adopted child hadn't even let me finish teaching her to read.

I found, however much I drank, I couldn't stop being sober, so I went miserably to bed, to lie queasily awake with 'Peter Pan' propped open on my belly, absorbed in aimless verbal abuse and self-pitying regrets, just like old times.

Two days later, though it now seemed only like clambering through dreary hoops and lolloping over tedious hurdles in a one-woman race I would be certain to lose, I finally shook off my lethargy and made my way, tortoise-like, to the beach. I stood on the cliff top by the old Sailors' Reading Room and looked down, knowing there would be no one, not even a stray mad policeman or a drunken sailor, to welcome my return.

There is a wide promenade at Southwold beach, and blocks of wooden huts painted in ice-cream colours are lined up like a street in Legoland along the walkway, over a mile long (I should know, I've walked it in pirate costume often enough). I'd looked forward to showing Kyra this, telling her about the dear dead times, the changeable summers of the early twenty-first century, the North London kiddies in their Boden teeshirts and suntops, the biddable, well-nourished regular customers who knew all the jokes and came running at the clamour of our Pied Piper's bell. Sometimes Guy took the drum, and parents complained about the noise, and he whacked it louder anyway, all the way to the jazzed-up, pastel-painted pier and back.

Our old British racing green beach hut, leaning at the same politely drunken angle as always, welcomed my approach, door flapping. Last time I'd been inside – last time I really looked at the inside of the place – it had been crammed tightly with props, costumes, musical instruments, whisky bottles and wrappers from the ice-creams Guy and I had shored ourselves up with on those days when the show must go on regardless of hangovers, slipped discs, marital tiffs, gale warnings and invasions of tambourine-smacking evangelists with their competing 'make a Christian sandcastle' competitions.

> *'Well, I thought I heard the old man say,*
> *Leave her, Johnny, leave her,*
> *It's a long hard pull to the next pay-day*
> *And it's time for us to leave her . . .'*

My voice thinly, reedily, wafts into the windless winter air. I hear the rumbling crash of far-off waves, always moving, never getting there.

~

Sally has made a decision. She's moved house. She didn't like stepping over the mess on her front path, even though the Tesco gang took most of the body with them to display to the rest as a warning against soft-heartedness, which nowadays, everyone agrees, endangers survival. They didn't, naturally enough, mop up the semi-liquid bits and until it rained Sally was stuck with them, so she moved into another house two doors away – exactly the same house, really, only not hers. It doesn't feel right, even though she's installed a few intimate possessions – there's even the same kitchen cupboard for her to put the hospital bottle in. With that and a newspaper and a few onion skins she's well set up. A lot better off than some people. Even if there isn't one calorie of food in the place.

I haunted our old beach hut for a few days, wondering what to do next. Sylvia had been right; things were shifting. One night I was sure I saw the street lamps flicker on, just for a moment Or maybe it was a flash of lightning.

I visited all the empty shops but never saw a soul. Southwold people, I already knew from a brief and unrewarding spell as Town Crier, were generally self-sufficient and undemonstrative in that East Anglian way that comes from being out on a geographical limb. Undemonstrative, yes – that was why Guy and I felt so at home here.

If I'd been really tough, I could have gone back to our old cottage, or moved base to somewhere nearer the sea front, but then I thought of Kyra – let's face it, I was thinking about Kyra most of the time when I wasn't thinking about Guy – so I stayed put, just in case.

I notice I seem to have stopped eating since Kyra left. I don't seem to have the same bestial old physical needs I used to. I like this refinement of the senses, this etherealisation. But it suggests to me that my time is running out.

I'd looked all the way along the beach. The main street. St. Edmund's Church – not, in my book, a crowd-pleaser like Blythburgh – and Gun Hill. Finally, I heeded that H for Hook sign, and went to the hospital. I'd been pretending to myself that it was the one place Guy wouldn't be, which was convenient, but untrue.

Hated hospitals, he always had. Hadn't he funked it, made himself scarce, made the nurses shake their heads sympathetically when I said I had no one to visit me? I'm being cowardly here. What they actually asked was, 'Where's the father?'

When you make a puppet, you surround yourself with little boxes of flexible wire and foam rubber chippings, scraps of material, old tobacco tins full of tiny glass eyes, fur that can be made into very convincing hair, and bits of suede and leather for shoes and latex for the skin . . . Out of that, you stitch and glue a little creature you can, later on, give a name and a voice to, as you breathe life into it.

Well, that's the stage I had been at, the assembly stage.

I went to my old ward. There'd been five of us in there, five failures in the motherhood arena, five women who ran the gamut of emotions – I chose A, others went all the way to Z – reluctantly forced to be part of the world of maternity until they'd healed up sufficiently to fly away home, like Lost Girls to Neverland. There was the corset-pink cupboard, still by my old bed, where the nurse had propped Guy's card, until I asked her to take it down and hide it, where my friends (thank God I'd still had some) had put the grapes and flowers when they visited, trying not to ask me too many questions. But, in truth, so much had happened since I was here last, that nostalgia hardly got a look in.

I wandered in a trance of numbness and detachment through the wards, wondering what part they might have played during the Eppie. There weren't many; some had evidently been re-opened and used for triage in a last-ditch British attempt to rekindle that wartime spirit of make do and mend.

Upstairs there was evidence of virile, assertive life; shit, graffiti, scorch marks, pools of urine.

At the end of the corridor was a closed door. I opened it, of course.

'Hello,' said Guy.

NINE

THE MEN ON THE INTERIM COMMITTEE have their various fingers on the pulse of the nation: energy, communications, transport, human resources management. Rodney was unclear about the last and had to have it explained. Everyone is to be registered 'voluntarily', but later on, those who have not registered will be denied food – which will be requisitioned into Army-controlled depots – and issues of the new identity cards, which will come later, without which you will not officially exist. A skeleton Army will double as police force.

'Human resources management' also includes disposal of bodies hygienically in burial pits. The term 'parped' is to be made illegal as it shows disrespect. Under this heading also are religious affairs, criminal and civil law, organised sport, social welfare and education.

Rodney sees, he understands, what a unique opportunity they have been given to put things – including his urges – that had got out of control back into proper order; to ensure a culture of discipline and obedience; to take control of population growth, the environment, energy, and of course, the internet. Numbers of survivors are so small that organising them, confused and starving as they are, will be child's play. All Rodney has to do is sign documents and make speeches, which will be written for him. To his relief, he is not asked to think.

He does, however, come up with an original idea during a meeting of the Communications Committee, or Comcom.

He has to wait a long time until the Chair motions him to speak, and when he does, how his voice quavers! It's the first time he's had a chance to show that he is more than a figurehead, that he believes in their future one hundred per cent.

'It struck me that when the official broadcasts begin, it would be a marvellous idea if we had a – moment each day. For good news. Stories of – oh, people helping each other? Maybe even heroism under adversity. So our people can begin to feel proud of themselves. And lucky to have survived.'

There's a buzz of approval round the table, as if they haven't already thought of this themselves.

'Jolly good, Leon,' says the Chair, 'we'll put that in the minutes.'

Guy and I stare at each other, absorbing changes. The news, from where I stand, does not look too cheerful.

Then Desmond's head pops up on the pillow.

'Hallo dere Billie, how are ye, and the top of the mornin' to ye,' he begins, and then the grimacing little face stops still, mouth dropping open.

'Do we have to talk with that thing listening?'

'Depends what you want to talk about,' says Guy, whose voice is, like his face, pale and moribund. He's hardly got any hair at all – and it used to be so pretty. Guy won't look at me. It's Desmond, as always, who does the talking. And he doesn't look at me either, but at his natural father.

'So, she's back. Why did she come back?'

'To haunt you,' I say. 'Both of you, if that's the way you want it.'

I sit on the bed – oh, not to establish contact. I suddenly feel the exhaustion of remembered rage.

'Ooh children, doesn't she look pissed off,' says Desmond chirpily, 'I expect she's remembering the . . .'

I'm remembering the beach hut that day, as the sun was slanting across the cliffs and all the tired children had been taken home. The day I thought would end with amazed kisses and champagne, that actually ended with a one way ticket and a drowning.

'That television producer, what was his name?'

Desmond does a take on Guy, who winks back at him, then Desmond wrinkles his nose, shrugs his insubstantial puppet shoulders—

'We didn't catch his name, we had a job to do at the time—'

'Yeah, a blow job. You bastard—'

'Please, not in front of the child,' says Guy, and his skull face is grinning as he pretends to cover Desmond's elfin ears.

'That's not a child – it's not alive, it's a freak, a bloody stupid puppet, it's not even well made, it's ugly and cheap—'

Desmond, only slightly ruffled, tilts his head in sparrowlike reproach: 'Oh, dear me; Lola's been at those Women's Lib tablets again—'

'I'm not Lola, you sponge. Lola is dead. Just like you will be when I've finished with you.'

'Temper, temper. No need to be unpleasant.' His head tilts to one side, birdlike again, but now a curious, malicious corvid, as he eyes me directly. 'I'm more indestructible than you are. And I've got the fan mail to prove it.'

'Shut him up, take him off your hand. I don't want him to talk. I want *you* to talk. I want to talk to you.'

'Oh, dear. We are demanding,' says Guy in his natural voice, which is whispery now, soft and tired. 'I'm afraid we don't do talking. We prattle, we jest, we rabbit on. But we don't do talking.'

That other, prelapsarian afternoon, centuries ago, we'd finished the two shows and packed up the booth, and although a few mad fans or punters were still hanging around trying to help, I escaped down to the sea. I was knackered, but luxuriated in the friendly nudgings of that tiredness, because it meant something bizarrely creative was afoot. Something I had never planned to happen had decided to happen, and now it had been secretly and uniquely confirmed to me, I realised it was a thing I was cautiously pleased about, and I vaguely assumed Guy would be too, when I told him.

A swim would be the discreet way to celebrate. A swift and definitely non-amniotic caress of the briskly unsentimental North Sea, where the blobby jellyfish brushed against my legs, nauseatingly like raw eggs, and twenty minutes getting the brain bashed out of me by waves, was more than enough.

A little dizzy, I climbed back up the hills of shingle to our beach hut, where we stored our stuff, where there might be some tea still in the thermos, and found the door was shut – something was jammed against it from the inside; as I pushed, it opened, reluctantly.

Guy and a man, lying naked on the bleached, gritty wooden floorboards of the hut – and Desmond was there too, unspeakably yet inevitably present and odiously active.

It was Desmond, as ever, who did all the talking on that occasion.

I grab the metal frame of Guy's bed and start shaking it as rage wells up, and I let it; this time I let the floodgates open and the black waters close over my head. My brain limps behind, reproachful, hesitant. Guy lies back, on his face that infuriating little smirk he has replicated so well on the latex features of his repellent, undersized alter ego. Shaking the bed isn't enough, it doesn't do the job at all, he can hardly feel it, so, suddenly, my hands are flailing, punching, pulling at his thin hair, smacking his faithless, secret, self-sufficient face to try and bring home to him how much I want to hurt him back . . .

'Sense and fucking sensibility!' is the best my brain can manage as I launch myself on his punished body, hoping by the weight of my fury to crush the breath out of him, crush him as I should have done that day I turned and walked away. But it's still not enough. It's like kicking a dream; my body has no force, except the force of feeling, and that is nearly spent. I lunge, grunting like a walrus, for his hand, I wrench the bastard child off his fingers and, before his startled eyes, I tear Desmond limb from limb. He splits right down the middle with a most satisfying, classic BBC-Radio-play-sound-effect rending noise. I shred him, I disembowel him, I excoriate him. I pull off his nose, claw at his bright button eyes, and finally take the smile off his face.

At last, Guy is, perhaps, beginning to feel something. But he wouldn't be Guy if he didn't then say, 'So you're a bit pissed off with us, then?'

'Not "us", just you,' I pant, dropping the shredded remains on the floor. 'Desmond isn't real. Desmond didn't fuck a TV producer. You can call your wretched little creation dead. I'd rather think of it as a dismembered dolly with no future waggling potential.'

Not a very punchy exit line, I agree, but there's no time for retakes. Magnificently, I turn, managing not to overbalance, I stride the length of the ward, and I open the door. I am exiting his life. For ever.

'Billie,' he says quietly, 'please. Don't go away.'

TEN

A FEW DAYS LATER – we didn't have a diary – a jeep came cruising gingerly up the main street and soldiers broke down the door of the old Lloyds Bank, establishing an Army H.Q. The soldiers were a mixture, hatchet-faced old regular survivors and sleepy, half-starved recruits without proper uniforms or weapons.

Those wary, astute native Southwoldians came slowly awake, like characters from 'Sleeping Beauty'. Out of their hiding places they crept, relieved that someone was taking charge. In return for surrendering looted food and weapons, they were given drinkable water, dried milk, tea, and bread. The soldiers' orders were to behave in a low-key, non-violent, informal manner; to win over the population. In sleepy, sluggish Suffolk this worked like a dream. Old ladies broke down and kissed them. Ex-gangs surrendered, asking if they could join up. Altogether about twenty people paid them a visit on that first day in Southwold.

In their gleaming Army jeep they toured the streets with a megaphone, announcing that everyone should switch on their radio or television that night at nine o'clock. Electrical power would be connected for two hours. Later in the week, everyone would have running water.

These smiling Army lads, who could look forward to a hot, freshly-cooked meal that night, were not allowed to answer questions about the Government, political parties, the Royal Family, the head of state, or national defence; but the relieved citizens were given to understand that all these remote administrative matters were once again in the hands of experienced, competent professionals. Elections were not on the agenda; anyone who mentioned the word 'democracy' had their photo taken and details filed, without their permission or knowledge.

That night, in the hospital, the electric lights came on as promised, and stayed on for half an hour.

Guy misses this exciting landmark in our post-plague evolution; he sleeps most of the time.

As he's obviously too ill to move, even back to my former des. res. on Pier Road, (though I still visit once a day, and have left Kyra a big sign with her name, which is all she can read, in case she comes back), I have looted the old place for duvets, pillows and orange juice and sleep next to him on an iron bed. So what if Desmond and Lola, latex rulers for five years of our tiny puppet empire, were split asunder in one naked revelation that afternoon, leaving Lola rejected and redundant, and her dollywaggler, now a solo act, free to walk back to the shore and drown her, slowly, in grey North Sea waves, tying her little dress down with beach pebbles. Imagine how hard it is to drown what is basically a rubber bath toy? But I, her maker, did it. And as Guy travelled first class to London, I walked away from Southwold beach, determined never to look back. The nobility of poverty I hugged to myself. Television? Selling out. Fame? Puppeteers aren't designed for it. Money? Pah!

Guy is incurious about my present, or our painful past, and only wants to hear about my journey from London. He loves the stories about Dennis the mad policeman, and Dave the Sultan of Saxmundham. I try and make Paradise Farm funny, but it doesn't work so well. It would be okay if they were still alive, but it seems cheap now, to make fun of their magnificently generous loopiness. And I can hardly bring myself to talk about Kyra, whom I was so careless as to lose.

'They had mad notions and believed in trees and goddesses and all kinds of wonky stuff. But they – they lived. They didn't just let life happen to them. They got stuck in; they died knowing they'd really, really got deep into things.'

'Things?' says Guy.

'Stuff.'

'Stuff?'

'Okay.' I bite the bullet. He can laugh all he likes. They were my friends. 'They knew how to feel. They weren't like us. And now they've all gone, I miss them being around, being not like us.'

Guy's not laughing.

'They knew how to love.'

Rodney, or rather Leon, impeccably attired and perfumed, sips from his glass of Malvern water. A message chirps through from the gallery. Ready to go transmission; start the clock.

He greatly approves of the content of his speech, which is a relief to him personally, and they were all very pleased with the way it went in rehearsal. Ten seconds to go. Suddenly, there's a last minute change of script – something about

Regional Commissioners. Leon nods like an old trouper: unflappable, rock-solid. He is completely sound.

~

I had found a telly in the Pier Road house and wheelbarrowed it all the way to Guy's private ward. At a time that I had to take on trust was exactly nine o'clock, Big Ben appeared and struck (library footage, probably). A faceless, reassuring, masculine voice announced:

'There will now be a short broadcast by Leon Buckmaster, the Prime Minister. This will be repeated tomorrow. Please watch and listen carefully. Your survival and happiness depends on everyone's understanding and co-operation. Thank you.'

'What did you mean, "sense and sensibility"?' Guy asked me, with amazingly bad timing.

'Ssh, I'm watching. Anyway, she married him, in the end.'

'Who married who?'

'Elinor married the rat. Edward. I don't feel the same way about Elinor any more. She could have shown a bit more spirit. When Edward gets the heave-ho from Lucy, all he did was go back and grovel a bit to Elinor, and she swallowed it! She "forgives" him. And they live happily ever after.'

Against a muted background of dark maroon wallpaper hung with eighteenth-century sporting prints, the face of the new Prime Minister, world-wise, solid and kindly, looked out at his new subjects.

'Guy, don't go to sleep. Look at this.'

He shakes himself awake, and scans at the screen with a disillusioned, camera-wise eye. 'My God, who's she?'

'The new Prime Minister. Leon something.'

We watch, interested in spite of ourselves.

'Who's working him?' he says, after a few minutes. 'Who's the dollywaggler?'

Is this it, then, living happily ever after, marrying sense to a modicum of sensibility?

Am I '*happily disposed, as is the human mind, to be easily familiarised with any change for the better*'? And is Guy '*elevated at once to that security with another, which he must have thought of with despair, as soon as he had learnt to consider it with desire*'?

Seems so.

There's an elephant in the room, though. A little baby one with big ears, a bit like Dumbo. It occasionally slaps me with its trunk.

~

At Paradise Farm, the new tenants have dragged in from somewhere an unbroken telly; now it's in the sitting room, positioned so that Mart gets the best view, his lieutenants, ranked around him, elbowing the uppity peasantry to the back row.

Amongst these are Amber and Clover, looking rather different now. Clover is dirty, foul-mouthed, and pregnant, although she doesn't know this yet; after Mart had finished with her, she went the rounds until she became someone's slit. There won't be any proof the baby is his; if he decides not to acknowledge it, which would be very bad luck for her, she'll get passed on again down the food chain, one of the tribal slits. Amber showed more fight and had to be starved into submission, so she looks anorexic, which in the old days Lally would have known how to deal with – counselling, massage, polarity therapy, and so on. Her face looks old and wrinkled; she now has no front teeth at all; they got knocked out by a blow from a car tyre lever, which also broke her nose. She's very quiet these days, and scratches continually at a bubbling eczema rash on her face, a nervous rash; and no one wants to know her, except Clover, but they meet in secret. They're developing a code too obscure for anyone else to follow, they're making up some rules for their future, and they have realised at last what the secrets were that the grown-ups used to whisper.

They heard about how an example was made of Gwyn, and Amber saw what they did to the bodies of her old family before Mart took her upstairs to the bed where Rose and Jamie used to sleep, and by using some of Jerry's old visualisation techniques, she coped with it.

But there is something they both know now, something that no one can take away. They chose life, and this means they have a spark, something vital that cannot be extinguished. They're learning fast. They don't have hearts; they don't tell anyone their thoughts. They can see that this group contains the seeds of its own destruction. They will be ready for whatever comes next.

What comes next is a flashing, a blinking of the screen as the picture gradually settles, and when the new National Anthem surges up, there is a hoarse cheer from the assembled citizens. Silence would be too much to ask for – but it's as quiet as it's been since the day of the parley as they listen to Leon, their new leader.

'. . . when the crisis began, the then government initiated a system of voluntary vaccination, which unfortunately turned out to be unsuccessful in a large number of cases. Those who refused the treatment were put into a special category, known as Refusals. Some of these were housed in holding camps and, as we probably remember, came to be known as "Refs". I believe that society would not have survived as successfully as it has done today if the then Government had not made these difficult decisions about putting us into social categories for our own good at that time of grave worldwide crisis. However, this crisis is now over, and as a result, "Refs" as a category will cease to exist.

Any social stigma which may be felt by any of this surviving minority is to be immediately eradicated by a programme of free designation removal, for those who—'

'Woss'ee mean?'

'Torch your tattoo off, stupid wanker—'

'Do we 'ave to?'

'Listen what he's saying, you pillock—'

After the broadcast, for a while, no one notices that Mart has gone. He is on the black horse, galloping, galloping and his destination, like his destiny, is London.

~

'... internationally, we are beginning to pull together the threads of a world-wide network ...'

Guy is nodding off, but this jerks him awake. 'Was the plague in Ireland too?'

'Of course.'

'Galway? Where you were?'

'Yes.'

'But you didn't get it?'

'Does it matter? I'm here.'

'So you were immune? So you got on the last plane or ferry or whatever?'

Now we're getting close. 'I think I died.'

'And?'

'Someone gave me a second chance.'

Guy smiles, then tries not to. 'Sorry. It's not funny. Just that – those hippies have got to you more than you think.'

'. . . very soon we shall be providing tap water to all the major cities in most areas of the United Kingdom. Rural areas will have regular deliveries, which for the time being will be free of any charge . . .'

Guy looks at me, really looks, for the first time. 'Come here. I can't see you properly.' He holds my chin in his good hand. 'For a ghost, you look disgracefully robust to me.'

'. . . finally, let me say that there is something that each and every one of you can do. In these past terrible weeks, we have all seen dreadful things. Some of us have done things we are ashamed of . . .'

In the new house, which never felt like home, Sally's television has come alive, its friendly flickering livening the walls of the yellow-papered sitting room. She is not watching; she is not in the kitchen, she is not in the house.

She is on the banks of the river, by the waters of Babylon. She is standing at the water's edge, but this time she has not come here to swim. Nor to sing. One hand grips the neck of the hospital bottle, empty now, drained to its dregs.

She watches a gull with something pink dangling from its

beak gazing alertly across the water. A cold eye meets hers, the beak jerks and the pink tidbit disappears. Wouldn't she rather be at home, watching telly?

Her arm swings down, suddenly and with force smacking the bottle hard against a rough stone; the end cracks off, leaving a splintered edge of glass to which an antiseptic smell still clings. She drops to her knees, shuffling into the water, trying to make herself small, as if it mattered now whether anyone sees her or not . . .

Underwater is best. Her streaming wrists lie limp in the friendly, filthy tide, her flesh blue-white as a mermaid's, the raw redness and the black of the rotting mud all gone now, all clean. Sally sighs, closing her eyes, and lets her body fall forward – falling, falling, easy and free, finally free.

⁓

'. . . now it is time to put all that behind us, as we remember that we are human beings, and I believe, here on earth, ultimately to love, help, and care for one another. Let us make a new beginning, a fresh start. The past is dead. We, the living, look to the future.'

'What a load of pants,' said Guy.

⁓

Alastair is sitting in his kitchen, in his particular chair, across from her chair, here, where he and Margaret used to watch 'Eastenders' while they ate supper together. Throughout the long speech, Alastair has been wavering. He doesn't see himself as quite the same decent man that saved Guy's life; he feels contempt for himself in his new incarnation, as an addict, a daily sampler of the remains of his medicine cupboard – but what was there for him after Margaret?

Now, he's a floating voter. Before the Eppie, his was a decent, contained life, a square life, a life true to his private principles, but those he now feels he has betrayed.

At the first sight of Buckmaster with his sagging, kindly roué's face, he had mentally voted no. This was merely re-setting the programme, the same tired old platitudes, the same corrupt pyramid.

Several times, he was about to switch off. But each time his hand moved towards the switch there was a phrase, a promise . . . an understanding. Gradually, he was won over. The man was talking reasonably. He understood the darkness, the underbelly. It even seemed as if he might have been a part of it. But if I can put that behind me, he seemed to be saying, so can you all.

As the final words of Buckmaster's speech faded, to be replaced by a gradually surging orchestral theme – a tear-jerkingly majestic tune that reminded him of 'Land of Hope and Glory', 'Jerusalem' and 'God save the Queen' (it was meant to) – Alastair felt tears prickling his eyes. He missed Margaret. He missed Greg. He missed Guy. He wanted the past, but he couldn't have the past, so he would buy this deal. Yes, he would buy in to this fragile, this fledgling future.

Congratulations are low-key, but sincere.

'. . . very persuasive . . .'

'. . . convincing and authentic . . .'

'. . . foresee no problems with Stage Five . . .'

'What is Stage Five?' asks Leon, timid as yet.

Sir Geoffrey adjusts Leon's tie. 'Re-establishment. Stage Four was Re-integration, which, thanks to you, is going to proceed very smoothly indeed.'

'What was the thing about Regional Commissioners?'

There is a perceptible souring of the atmosphere. Sir Geoffrey purses his lips and Leon feels a sinking in his stomach. At this stage, it could take so little . . . so very little . . .

'The regions are going to take a little longer to . . . integrate. Of course, there are the geographical . . .' other voices pick up the theme: '. . . purely an administrative . . .'

'. . . handful of political agitators, taking advantage . . .'

'... old nationalistic hangovers ... devolution clearly a mistake ...'

'They'll soon find out they can't exist in isolation.' Sir Geoffrey smiles. Leon notices a grey stain on his front tooth. 'So – I wouldn't lose any sleep over it, Prime Minister.'

Guy, still awake, holds my hand.

'Tell me, the – the – baby ... boy or girl?'

'Boy.'

'Did you ... see him?'

All I see now is Ross, sucking on that delicious, lethal ruby bottle.

'No. They said he – he – was perfect. Too perfect to live, it would seem.'

Oh, what a bad move that had been. Trying to avoid pain, when they offered me a dead baby to hold and gaze at, they'd suggested a ceremony, a burial place, a memorial, I'd chosen the very options that now stab and pierce me as if the wound was yesterday's thing. What I was stupidly trying to do then was make it as if it had never happened.

'A baby boy,' says Guy. Oh no, please, no. A tear falls on my hand. I am breathing, breathing for dear life and sanity. His grip tightens. 'I am so sorry.'

He is, remarkably, crying. Crying really rather well, rather expertly, it would seem. And I have no breath left. I use a hospital sheet, when we're ready, to wipe our novices' tears. Is it possible that a pair of irredeemable old dollywagglers, resolutely committed to concealment, could have finally joined the human race?

Imagine if I had become a mother; I would have cried a great deal by now. Watching my baby getting sick, dying, or, even worse, forced to make the choice that Gwyn made, which, belatedly, I now recognise as brave. And from day one, from the first time he was put into my arms, I would have understood what it was to be vulnerable.

'If I had only known—'

But I, quite kindly and gently, stop his mouth. That is more than enough of what might have been. He slides into sleep. He breathes very slowly now when he sleeps, with long gaps in between. Cheyne-Stokes breathing, Sally would have called it. When he goes, I am sure I will go too. I am attempting not to be afraid.

The television began to broadcast every night. At six o clock, after the news, there was a spot called '*My Miracle*'. Ordinary survivors from all around the country started telling their stories, of extraordinary deeds of kindness, heroism, luck, etc. Stories about those who had caught the plague, fought it, and lived.

'There you are, you see,' said Guy, 'you're not the only one.'

'No. I *was* dead. I know I was. The lights came after I was dead. They had a plan for me, they were telling me what to do.'

'Totally wrong. They weren't there to give you what they wanted, they gave you what *you* wanted,' says Guy, which seems to me, perversely, less desirable.

'How do you know so much all of a sudden? They were my invisible beings, not yours. I didn't want to lose Kyra. Suppose I don't want you to die?'

'Don't push your luck, you only get one go,' he says, infuriatingly right, as ever.

He died in the early hours of the next morning, and I lit the four candles I had brought with me around him, as they did in Ireland for all the plague victims. So, had I known there would be a reconciliation? What had I hoped for? He said no memorable last words to me. Nor, in fairness, did I to him, because I was asleep until the cessation of his laboured breathing woke me.

I tucked the sheets and blankets around him, I kissed his cold cheek for the last time, and of course, a song came, though I did not seek it . . .

I dreamed a dream the other night,
Lowlands away . . .
I dreamed my love came standing by . . .
Lowlands, lowlands away, my John,
Came standing close to my bedside,
Lowlands away.
He's drowning in the Lowlands low . . .

I wait then, for me to be taken too. Wasn't that the deal?

I wait for my breath to falter, my steady heartbeat to slow and stop, my skin to grow cold as any stone.

Guy looks peaceful, his skin tone pale-pink-putty, uniform, unwrinkled, inexpressive; maybe he's allowed to leave the studio floor now, stretched out forever on a couch in some celestial dressing-room, with a bucket of heavenly champagne chilling at his elbow. I wonder, fleetingly, if there's a shadowy Desmond waiting for him up there too.

The candles flicker. Are they here now, those angels? Have they come to bear me away on their snow white wings to my immortal home? Clearly, my business here on earth is done.

Five minutes later:

Er – so what am I doing, still apparently here on earth?

A voice, Kyra's, I think, says, 'H for Hook'.

I spin around, but she's not there.

'H is for Hospital,' I say out loud. And, with a sudden tug

at my (evidently still very solid) guts, I see her, trudging along the roads, trudging W for west. I see her reluctantly, because the struggle to make sense of it all is not over for me, not as long as she is out there, somewhere.

Say I don't find her? There will, surely, be other children without parents, other babies needing mothers.

I leave Guy, and the ward, and with nothing in my pack, I head West.

I'll find her. Or die in the attempt.

EPILOGUE

THAT SHOULD HAVE BEEN IT, leaving the chunky, misanthropic old dollywaggler a better and altogether much nicer person – alive, it would seem, and fairly bursting with the syrup of universal love and irritatingly unquenchable optimism, but still mapless; without a clue, really.

I walked for the last time along the coast road, above the beach. As the day faded, the sea, reliable as ever, was subtly joining its grey to the greying sky. Sound of heavy marine breathing, gasping and sighing rhythmically up and down the shingle.

From south to north, almost to the pier, I walked, thinking

of Guy, maybe looking down on me, maybe not. Thinking of everything we'd done and been together, and all the things we hadn't.

Passing Sylvia's house, I saw electric lights on. Oh, of course, the power was back now, two hours a night.

In my new incarnation as kindly, forgiving, trusting, ungrudging person able to befriend others, I knock on the door. Sylvia opens it, and in her face I see excitement, energy. Something has happened.

The next minute, a small figure hurtles along the corridor and throws itself, herself, into my arms.

'I found her,' says Sylvia, while Kyra, extraordinarily, is kissing me and hugging me with such force I can hardly take a breath, 'spent two days searching, found her in a boat, down by the harbour. She said she was going in the boat to find her friend – not you, not Billie, if that's you?'

They are dragging me, not the least bit reluctant, but as clumsy as ever, tripping over my feet and Kyra's, into the living room, where lights are blazing merrily. Something else has changed. All the photos have gone.

'We've decided,' says Sylvia, 'we're moving.'

Kyra pushes me down in an armchair and climbs on my lap.

She is transformed. Sylvia has washed and cut her hair, and given her a bath, and dressed her – ('She chose the clothes. She's so small for her age, she liked Gemma's things especially, I hope you approve?') I, approve? Since when has Kyra needed my approval for anything? But now, clean and smelling of apples, I see in her shining face the sweetest, faintest resemblance to Rose, to her mother. In her hair, the same tints of red-gold. Mm, seems like hair is actually rather important to morale and general cheerfulness.

'If you like, there's a shower, we've got water now,' says Sylvia, ever-tactful, 'but before that, come and see this.'

We go into the garage, where the little red van has sat since Eddie last parked it.

'I hadn't really looked carefully,' she says, and her lip trembles, but she's got guts, this straight lady, and she shakes the tears away. 'He thought of everything, really he did. Look.'

Under the piles of tins and packets, lie four ten-litre jerricans of petrol. Eddie, I take my hat off to you. What a gem you must have been.

'The tank's full. We could go anywhere,' says Sylvia, and she's talking rapidly now, before I have a chance to raise objections, 'because I noticed on the, you know, Prime Minister's speech, they said that the regions would have Commissioners in about a month, and you know what Eddie would say? Eddie was old Labour, through and through, and he hated – excuse my language – bullshit. He would say that they aren't in control of everywhere, this new lot, and that the regions are still free, and if there was hope, it's not here, where the Army is handing out those papers to everyone.'

Kyra is patting my face in a dreamy way.

'Yes, I'm real. And will we stay together now?' She nods, emphatic. 'And tell us, o wise little Kyra, where shall we go? '

'To my friend.'

'I've packed. I've got everything that matters in here,' says the astonishing Sylvia, showing me a nifty little suitcase on wheels with extendable handle.

I warm to Sylvia; she is *so* not a hippy.

'Kyra says I have to come too.' And Sylvia rests her case for the defence, which I am sure is packed with maximum efficiency.

'Tell us about this friend, Kyra, who is he and where does he live?'

'It is Gwyn's brother in Wales. Name is . . . Welsh. Hard to say it.'

Not too much to go on, then. But we know this much: Wales. We could make it to Wales, Kyra and Sylvia and me, unlikely trio that we are, in Eddie's van, unregistered refugees, beetles scrabbling optimistically below the radar of this new totalitarian state; heading W for West, W for Wales.

Gwyn's country, I realise, with a jolt of pain and pleasure;

a passionate small outpost of poetry and hope.

Because, it seems to me, if we want a future that has love in it, that is where it lies.

About the Author

Frances Kay was born in London last century. Her inside knowledge of dollywagglers and their world comes from long summers spent on the beach at Southwold with Nutmeg Puppet Company, and many happy seasons with BBC TV as ‘Cosmo’ on the early years’ programme YOU AND ME. Cosmo was an assertive Geordie female creature of no known species who lived in a utopian street market with her friend Dibs, a slightly less forceful London boy.

Also from Tenebris Books

Willow, Weep No More

Fairytales once held an important place in the lives of people of every age and social rank. Handed down from generation to generation like precious heirlooms, these stories told of the struggles between good and evil, rich and poor, and often culminated in an allusion to how we reap what we sow. They served both as social commentary and morality lessons, seasoned with magic spells, mythical creatures, and enchanted objects. However, their enduring appeal is perhaps not only in the fantastical journeys on which they take us, but in the fact that they allow even the lowliest of us to believe there is reason to hope and dream.

Willow, Weep No More is a collection of traditionally-inspired tales that capture the magic and charm of the fairytale realm, whilst seeking to explore the depths of human wisdom, beauty and strength.

Published November 2013

www.tenebrisbooks.com